EADAN'S VOW

HIGHLANDER FATE BOOK ONE

STELLA KNIGHT

PRONUNCIATION GUIDE

Eadan - AE-dan
Ronan - ROE-nan
Magaidh - MAG-ee
Dughall - DOO-ghul
Bran - BRAN
Uisdean - OOSH-jun
Naoghas - NOO-us
Maon - MOON
Sorcha - SAWR-khə

CHAPTER 1

Present Day
Aberdeen, Scotland

Fiona couldn't take her eyes off the painting. It depicted a stunning landscape from somewhere in the Scottish Highlands, rolling hills and mountains, a sprawling forest, and a pristine blue sky. Something about it drew her toward it, and she had an odd sense of déjà vu, as if she'd seen this painting before.

She blinked, pulling herself back to the present. She glanced around the tiny museum she'd found tucked away on a tiny side street in Aberdeen. Besides herself, there was a middle-aged English couple, a small group of bored-looking students with their enthusiastic teacher, and an elderly woman who kept casting surreptitious glances her way. They'd all passed this painting by; Fiona was the only one who seemed to notice it existence.

She turned her focus back to the painting, studying the label next to it: *1390, Scottish Highlands. Artist Unknown.*

"An art dealer in Edinburgh discovered this at an estate sale."

Fiona turned as the elderly museum owner, Callum, approached her with a smile.

"I knew there was something special about it," he continued.

"It's lovely," Fiona said politely, though she didn't want to get stuck talking to him. She'd already witnessed him trying to up sell kitschy souvenirs to the other tourists.

"Ah, an American," Callum said, before she could walk away. "Where are you from?"

"Chicago."

She decided not to mention that she was in Scotland for what was supposed to be her honeymoon. Only a few weeks ago, she'd called off her wedding after discovering her fiancé Derek cheating on her with his coworker. Fiona kept a polite smile pinned on her face, even as bitterness pierced her at the memory.

"Chicago. Lovely city I hear," Callum said. "Never been out of Scotland myself. Always hoped to one day go to America."

Fiona's phone chirped with a text—the perfect out. Relief flowed through her, and she gave Callum an apologetic look as she pointed to her phone, starting to step around him.

"Before you make your way out, perhaps you'd

like to explore the gift shop?" Callum asked, a mercenary gleam in his eyes.

Fiona stifled a sigh. He'd gotten her; he probably didn't care one bit about the painting. She cast one last look at it before trailing him to the adjoining gift shop, where she ended up buying several mugs and key chains she didn't need.

As she headed out of the gift shop with her stash of souvenirs, her skin prickled at the sensation of eyes on the back of her neck. Fiona turned.

Shock roiled through her. The same elderly woman who'd kept looking at her in the museum stood in the back of the gift shop. Only now, it looked as if she'd aged down by about ten years; she had fewer wrinkles and much of the gray strands in her hair had vanished, replaced with strands of black. And Fiona was certain it was the same woman.

"Can I help you with anything else?" Callum asked eagerly, as Fiona stood frozen by the open doorway.

"No," Fiona forced herself to say, before returning her focus to the woman. But the woman was no longer there. Fiona looked around, confused, but the woman was nowhere to be seen. "Have—have a good day."

What the hell was that all about? Fiona wondered in a daze, as she stepped out onto the street, making her way to her rental car. First, the painting that had mesmerized her, striking her with that sense of déjà vu, and then the female Benjamin Button.

She'd only been in Scotland for a few days, and nothing out of the ordinary had happened until today. It surprised Fiona how much she enjoyed the country. She'd never been here before, but it felt like she was returning home after a long absence. After Derek's betrayal, her best friend, Isabelle, had encouraged her to re-purpose this trip into a solo artist retreat of sorts. As an artist, she loved sketching and painting beautiful landscapes; Scotland had them in spades.

She'd started her trip here in Aberdeen, intending to make her way to the Highlands, where she'd stay in Inverness for a couple of days, before heading down to Glasgow and then Edinburgh, where she'd meet up with Isabelle. She planned to submit the landscapes she sketched here to an art show back in Chicago. Fiona taught art to high school students for a living, and unlike other art teachers she knew, she found her job fulfilling and enjoyed it—but sometimes she got the urge to put her works on display.

Fiona slid into her rental car, giving the museum one last glance before starting the car and driving away. She'd found it by accident after stopping for coffee at a nearby café. Despite the pushy owner, the strange woman, and the painting, she'd enjoyed visiting it and taking in the paintings and sculptures it had on display. It was the type of place Derek would have hated to visit; looking at art wasn't one of his favorite pastimes. Now that she thought about it, that wasn't a good sign.

She scowled as she recalled Derek's dismissiveness of her art. He'd urged her to go into graphic design instead, insisting she'd make more money and wouldn't have to teach. Her insistence that she liked the good old-fashioned raw materials of sketching and painting had fallen on deaf ears. But Derek hadn't been the best listener. *Or the best fiancé*, she thought, with a wave of bitterness.

She'd discovered his cheating in the most cliché of ways. With the date of their wedding getting closer, things had become oddly tense between them. They'd gotten into a terrible fight over the guest list, and Fiona had gone to his apartment, prepared to offer him an olive branch. And that's when she'd found him in bed with Karen, his coworker whom Fiona had never liked.

Looking back, what surprised her the most was her utter lack of heartbreak. She'd been humiliated, she'd cried, and she'd yelled at him when he called with pathetic excuses, but she'd not felt the level of devastation one should feel after discovering such a betrayal.

Derek had often accused her of not fully opening herself up to him, and maybe there was some truth to that. Her parents had died in a car accident when she was five, and she'd been raised by her kind yet distant Aunt Carol. Carol had died when she was in college, and ever since she'd developed the bad habit of isolating herself; closing herself off to relationships. Her relationship with Derek was an attempt to change this. So when Derek proposed after two years of dating, she'd accepted. She was twenty-eight, Derek thirty, it just seemed like the logical next step for them.

But something had never felt quite . . . right between them. Their lovemaking was okay, their relationship . . . fine, but there hadn't been the *fire* she always imagined she'd feel when she met The One. Hell, she'd felt more of a pull toward that landscape painting than to her ex-fiancé.

By the time she pulled into the parking garage of her hotel, she decided to put the strange encounter at the museum behind her, along with all thoughts of her ex. She entered the candlelit lobby, averting her eyes from at least two couples engaged in full-on PDA. Her hotel was a romantic destination for honeymooners and couples; she'd had to make a rather humiliating phone call asking them to downgrade her room to a standard one from the honeymoon suite, and they'd obliged her without too many questions.

She entered her hotel room, catching a glimpse of herself in the mirror. Her chestnut brown hair had escaped from its loose bun during her drive, returning to its naturally unruly state somewhere between wavy and curly. Her light brown eyes were shadowed, and she wearily rubbed at them. Encountering that painting—and the strange woman—at the museum had affected her more than she'd thought.

She sighed, tossing her bag of useless souvenirs onto the bed. She'd already bought too many souvenirs; at this point she'd have to buy another suitcase before she left. At the thought of leaving Scotland, a sudden sadness filled her. She dreaded leaving this beautiful country with its lush landscapes, kind people, and most importantly, its long distance from Chicago—Ground Zero of her broken engagement.

Her phone rang and she glanced down at it: Isabelle. The incident at the museum had distracted her so much, she'd forgotten Isabelle had texted.

"Do you love Scotland or do you love Scotland?" Isabelle asked, as soon as Fiona answered.

Fiona grinned at Isabelle's enthusiasm. Without Isabelle's influence, Fiona would have canceled the trip altogether.

"I have to say, you were right. I love it," Fiona said. "I'm glad I came. When did you get in?"

"Late last night. I'm a little jet-lagged," Isabelle said, stifling a yawn, "but I can't wait to meet up with you after I do the obligatory family meet up."

"Tell Scott I said hi," Fiona said. Isabelle's brother Scott and his wife lived in Edinburgh.

"I will. And, um, he may have a couple of friends he'd like to introduce you to," Isabelle hedged.

"No way," Fiona said. Isabelle had been on her case to get a rebound ever since she'd told her of Derek's betrayal. But Fiona had no intention of doing so. After the Derek disaster, she was content to be on her own. Maybe she was better off alone.

"Well. If said friends *happen* to be at a bar we were to visit . . ." Isabelle continued, her tone mischievous.

"I'm not here to have a fling, Isabelle," Fiona said, scowling. "Solo artist retreat, remember? Me time, remember?"

"Doesn't mean you can't have fun," Isabelle said innocently.

"Isabelle—"

"OK, OK. I'll tell my brother—and his wife—to lay off. Tell me what you've been up to so far," Isabelle said with a sigh.

Fiona told her about the museums she'd visited and some cityscapes she'd already sketched. She left out today's incident at the museum. She didn't even know how she'd describe what happened. *I saw a painting that hypnotized me and an old woman reverse aged in the span of minutes. I may or may not be losing my mind.*

After Isabelle yawned the fifth time, Fiona urged her to get some rest and ended the call.

Isabelle was a fellow teacher from her school and they'd become fast friends, even though they were total opposites. Isabelle was loud, feisty, and opinionated, Fiona more reserved. As she looked down at her phone, she wondered if she should have told Isabelle about the painting, and the de-aging woman at the museum. Isabelle was logical to a fault; she'd have a reasonable explanation.

Fiona shook her head, telling herself that they were both mere coincidences; odd blips on an otherwise ordinary trip to Scotland. But a nagging part of her couldn't help but suspect they were linked.

CHAPTER 2

1390
Macleay Castle

The cheers and laughter that surrounded Eadan grated at his ears. He forced a smile and raised his cup of ale as a distant cousin shouted words of congratulations from across the hall. At his side, Magaidh, his bride-to-be, wore a strained smile that must have matched his own. Eadan met her eyes, stiffening at the hatred he saw lurking in their green depths, before she quickly lowered them. His bride-to-be seemed to hate this arrangement as much as he did.

The grand hall of Macleay Castle was more crowded than usual, filled with various members of two formerly feuding clans, Clan Acheson and Clan Macleay. They were all gathered to celebrate his betrothal to Magaidh, the daughter of the

Acheson chief. Eadan sat at the head table with Magaidh and other leading nobles of the two clans.

He looked out at the great hall. Light from the various candles and two large fireplaces that were on opposite ends of the hall illuminated the cheerful faces of the guests. Several servants moved to and fro, carrying trays of wine and ale to refill their cups. The boisterous conversation of the guests filled every corner of the vaulted great hall. Eadan studied their jovial faces, wishing he could share the same cheer.

"Christ, Eadan." Eadan stiffened as Ronan, seated on his opposite site, hissed the oath in his ears. "At least try tae seem like ye're happy about this. That smile looks painful."

Eadan turned to scowl at Ronan. Ronan was his cousin; Eadan's father Bran had raised him as his own after the death of Ronan's father. There weren't many members of their clan who could get away with talking to Eadan, the *tainistear*—the chief's heir—the way Ronan did.

Eadan decided not to reply, worried that Magaidh's keen ears would pick up on whatever he said. His gaze slid back to her as she sipped her wine. She was a lovely woman, with long auburn hair and vibrant green eyes, but Eadan wasn't one to be taken by mere beauty—she was as cruel as a viper. He'd witnessed how she treated the castle servants, as if they were no better than rodents scampering at her feet. If Eadan hadn't intervened, she would have gotten an elderly cook who'd worked at the castle since he was a bairn dismissed for not cooking her supper the exact way she liked. He knew Magaidh hated him, though she tried to hide her dislike behind coquettish smiles. A part of him felt sorry for her; daughters of high-ranking clan members rarely had a choice when it came to their husbands, but he suspected Magaidh wasn't so innocent.

"Tae Eadan and my beloved daughter," a voice boomed.

Eadan turned to face the man who spoke at the opposite end of their table—Dughall, Magaidh's father. He had the auburn hair, now shot through with gray, and green eyes that his daughter shared. For a man in his late fifties, he was still sturdy and strong. He'd been a strong fighter in his youth, and he remained an expert swordsman to this day.

Dughall lumbered to his feet, his smile forced as he raised his cup of ale.

"May yer lives be fruitful after ye wed."

"Aye!" the guests cried, as Dughall took his seat again, his eyes never leaving Eadan's, and he could have sworn he saw a dark look in the older man's eyes.

Their two clans had been feuding for years over a disputed patch of land in the northern Highlands. Dughall was the one who'd approached his father with a peace offering. He wanted to join their clans in marriage; his daughter and only heir Magaidh, to Eadan, heir to Clan Macleay.

But the offer had struck Eadan as odd. Until

recently, Dughall had been a vocal proponent of going to outright war over the disputed land. It was only the calm diplomacy of his father that prevented Dughall from rousing the nobles to battle. Dughall had gone quiet over talks of war and suggested the betrothal only weeks later. It was an abrupt change of position, one that Eadan didn't trust.

Eadan's father Bran was a shrewd man, but he'd fallen ill in the past year, and was now a shadow of the strong man he'd once been. The castle healer had told Eadan he didn't believe his father had much time left; Eadan suspected Bran had taken Dughall's offer because of this—he wanted to leave this life knowing his clan could have peace.

When Eadan tried to argue with his father, telling him he found Dughall's peace offering suspicious, Bran had curtly told him that as chieftain of the clan, it was his right to accept such an offer, and had refused to listen to anything further Eadan had to say about the matter. Knowing how important ending the feud was to his father, and to the clan, Eadan had agreed to the betrothal, though his instincts that something was amiss remained.

Bran, seated at the center of their long table, rapped on the table for silence. The hall fell silent as his father lurched to his feet, leaning heavily on his cane.

"'Tis my honor tae join Clan Macleay and Clan Acheson with the betrothal of my sole heir, Eadan, tae Dughall's bonnie daughter Magaidh."

Bran turned to Eadan and Magaidh, raising his cup of ale. "May ye have strong sons and continue the peace for years tae come."

The hall erupted with cheers and Eadan struggled to keep the smile pinned on his face. As the cheers rose to a crescendo, Bran gestured for Eadan to stand.

Dread filled every part of him, but Eadan got to his feet, turning to face the guests.

"I look forward tae a long and fruitful marriage," he lied. "Tae the joining of our clans, and tae peace."

As the cheers and cries continued, Eadan's gaze landed on Dughall. This time, Eadan knew that he didn't just imagine the dark look in the man's eyes. Eadan's chest tightened; Dughall was hiding something, and he would find out what it was—before he married his daughter. Eadan kept his eyes trained on Dughall as he held up his ale and bellowed, "Tae peace!"

"Tae peace!" the guests echoed.

Eadan turned, gesturing for the minstrels to resume their music. Many guests stood, streaming to the center of the hall to dance. The ale and wine they'd consumed had taken full affect, and they were giddy with merriment.

At his side, Ronan gave him a meaningful look that said, "Ask your betrothed to dance." Eadan tensed, but turned to Magaidh.

"Would ye like tae join me for a dance?"

"Aye," she said, though her mouth tightened with dislike as he took her hand.

In a way, it was a relief that Magaidh hated him; if she fawned over him like a besotted maiden, it would make their betrothal—and marriage—even more difficult.

All eyes fell on them as they moved to the center of the hall to dance. Eadan's face had begun to hurt from the strained smile he wore, but he needed to look merry. He felt nothing as he pulled Magaidh into the circle of his arms to dance. Despite her beauty, there was no lust, no affection; not even hatred or dislike. He could have been dancing with air.

There were plenty of loveless marriages among the clan members, and he had no qualms about having one of his own. In fact, he preferred it. The men who loved their wives were distracted from their duties to the clan.

Though Bran was still chief of Clan Macleay in name, Eadan was laird of Macleay Castle, and he'd taken over his father's leadership duties as chief ever since he'd fallen ill. He wanted nothing more than to focus on leading the clan, overseeing the castle and his lands, without the distractions caused by love. He doubted he would even take a mistress as many husbands did. He would focus only on his role as laird and leader of his clan. And right now, his focus was on getting out of this betrothal—and figuring out what Dughall and his clan were up to.

CHAPTER 3

Present Day
Inverness and the Highlands, Scotland

iona left Aberdeen for Inverness early the next day, rolling down the window to let the fresh morning air flutter through her long brown hair as she drove. She was looking forward to exploring the Highlands; it was where she intended to get most of her sketching done.

She took in the stunning landscapes that surrounded her as she drove—the rolling expanses of flat grassy fields, punctuated by small towns or the ruins of old castles, the hazy outline of mountains in the distance, the stretch of clouds in the pristine blue sky. A tug of familiarity pulled at her, that same sense of déjà vu that seized her when she'd seen that painting. But she shook off the sensation; it was probably because she was enjoying her time here so much.

She arrived in Inverness a couple of hours later, checking into a quaint bed-and-breakfast on the outskirts of town, owned by a kind elderly married couple.

After settling in her room, she had her lunch in the small dining room of the bed-and-breakfast, where she realized with a stab of annoyance she was the only solo diner; once again, couples surrounded her. For the first time since she arrived in Scotland, a pierce of loneliness stabbed her heart. She wasn't lonely for Derek—or for any man—but there was something missing. It was a feeling that had plagued her over the years, even when she was with Derek; the sense that she'd misplaced something, something she'd lost, yet couldn't fathom what it was.

Fiona suddenly stilled, the sensation of eyes on her skin prickling the back of her neck. It was the same sensation she'd felt back at the museum in Aberdeen. She took a quick look around the dining room, but all the couples were engrossed in each other, and no one paid her any mind.

She swallowed, getting to her feet. Was she getting paranoid? She decided she needed to get some air, perhaps do some sketching. She'd intended to spend the day exploring Inverness, but decided instead to head out to the nearby town of Larkin, nestled in the midst of the Highlands, with plenty of breathtaking views. Sketching always relaxed her and helped take her mind off things.

It was still sunny out when she left. The bed-

and-breakfast owners told her a sunny day was a rare thing in Scotland, and to enjoy it.

As she drove out of Inverness and into the surrounding Highlands, a sense of calm and relaxation settled over her. She made a mental note to give Isabelle a big hug and thank her for convincing her to transform her honeymoon into a solo vacation; she didn't realize how much she'd needed it until now.

She was driving for about half an hour when she approached a forked road—the one on the left led to the town she was heading to, the one on the right led toward the mountains.

A sudden and inexplicable urge to turn right filled her, and Fiona gave into it, taking the road that veered right. She told herself that she'd briefly explore what was up ahead, then turn back around in a few miles.

The surrounding vistas were even more stunning here; the dark green hills and mountains that surrounded her spiraled into the sky toward clouds that blanketed the horizon, leaving only small patches of blue.

Fiona slowed down as she approached the ruins of what appeared to be a small medieval town, with several decrepit houses, and even a lone, aging castle in the distance.

She pulled over to the side of the road, looking down at the map on her phone, but there was no indication of any town here. She also checked the physical map she'd brought with her, and her guidebook, but they were both the same—no mention of the ruins of a medieval village.

Fiona got out of her car, looking around. There wasn't another soul in sight, and the main road she'd turned off of was miles behind her. In this moment, she felt like the only person in the world.

She took in the stunning vista that surrounded her, and knew she couldn't pass up the opportunity to sketch it.

Moments later, she found a comfortable sitting position on the ground and took out her pad to sketch. Soon, she became absorbed in her work, and everything else faded away. It was what she loved most about sketching or painting—the act took her out of place and time—it was what she did whenever she needed refuge from the stressors of everyday life.

When she finally looked up, her sketch almost complete, she blinked in astonishment. The sun hadn't moved, but she was certain that at least two hours had to have passed, which often happened when she got lost in her sketching.

She dug into her purse for her phone, glancing down at the time. And she froze.

It read the same time she'd arrived—2:15 p.m.

But that was impossible. She wondered if the dodgy cell reception of the Highlands made her cell's clock unreliable.

Fiona stood, heading to her car, and poked her head inside to look at the clock. But it read the same time. 2:15 p.m.

She shook her head, pushing aside her unease. Regardless of the time, she should head back to Inverness; she owed Isabelle a phone call. Reaching down, Fiona gathered her things, but she saw something out of the corner of her eye. Movement from the ruins of the castle.

Fiona straightened, studying the castle. She noticed the movement again. A woman. Though she was some distance away, Fiona could tell it was the same mysterious woman from the museum in Aberdeen.

Panic, fear and shock clawed its way through her chest. With a chill, Fiona recalled the sensation of eyes on her back at the bed-and-breakfast. *The woman was following her.*

Hot anger replaced her fear. Fiona dropped her things, stalking toward the castle.

"Hey!" she shouted, but there was no sign of the woman as she approached. "HEY!"

Fiona reached the ruins of the castle, stepping into the courtyard. She hesitated as another swell of déjà vu swept over her. This time the feeling was so overwhelming that she swayed on her feet. She looked around at the crumbling castle, unable to shake the sensation that she'd been here before. She swallowed as another chill crept up her spine.

Focus, Fiona. She needed to find that woman and find out what the hell was going on—and why she was following her. Fiona turned, scanning the courtyard. There was no sign of the woman, though she couldn't have gotten far.

"I know you're here! Why are you following me?"

She heard a scurry of movement coming from her left and turned. It had come from a crumbling tower; she could see a winding set of stairs leading below.

Fiona hurried toward it, making her way down the set of stairs, which was surprisingly solid compared to its crumbling surroundings. It led to what appeared to be an ancient, ruined cellar.

She looked around, disoriented. What if this was some sort of trap—and the woman had led her down here on purpose? Panic rising in her chest, Fiona turned back to head up the stairs, but the cellar had darkened, and she could barely see in front of her.

Taking deep breaths to calm herself, she found the wall with her hands, feeling along its rough surface to help guide her back to the entrance.

But she froze as a sudden rush of wind filled the cellar—as if a miniature invisible tornado had appeared. Her heart rate increased, and she tried to keep her grip planted on the wall to keep moving toward the entrance, but a tug of wind jerked her body back, away from the wall, and impossibly, she was *falling* . . .

CHAPTER 4

1390
Macleay Castle

*W*hen Fiona opened her eyes, she had a massive headache. Disoriented, she sat up, looking around at the dark cellar, momentarily forgetting where she was or how she'd gotten here.

And then it all came back to her. The mysterious ruins of the village, the woman who'd been following her, Fiona chasing her into the pits of the castle, the tug of wind, and the sensation of falling.

Fiona climbed to her feet, clutching her head. What had caused that wind? Maybe there'd been a sudden storm, and the rush of wind had caused her fall. Whatever had happened, she needed Ibuprofen, water, and a long nap back in her room at the bed-and-breakfast. If she saw that woman again, she'd just have to contact the authorities.

Though the cellar was still dark, Fiona could now see enough to make out the stairs up ahead. She blinked, taking in the cellar. It looked slightly different. It was larger, with no signs of decay. In fact, she saw barrels of wine and sacks of flour stacked in the far corner. Had someone been here?

Shaken, she made her way to the stairs, starting to ascend, but stilled when she heard two male voices.

"I'm telling ye, Ronan, they're up tae something. I doonae trust them."

"Yer father's wise, he wouldnae let Dughall fool him. Be happy with the lass, she's bonnie and will give ye strong sons—"

"'Tis not about Magaidh, 'tis about protecting the clan."

Fiona had heard thick, almost indiscernible Scottish accents since she'd arrived, but these sounded . . . different. Though she could understand them—barely—it was almost like they were speaking another language.

Other people are here, Fiona realized in a daze. When she'd arrived, the village had been a ghost town.

She climbed the stairs and froze when she reached the top.

Two handsome men stood in the corridor. They wore medieval-looking clothes—dark tunics and green plaid-patterned kilts. One was tall with brown hair, golden eyes, and strong angular features.

But it was the one who stood closest to her that made her throat go dry. He was tall, well over six feet, with dark wavy hair, cerulean blue eyes, and a finely chiseled jaw dotted with faint stubble. He was ridiculously, painfully gorgeous. A rush of heat spiraled through her, and she swallowed.

"Ah—sorry," she said, when she was able to speak. Maybe this was a historical reenactment? One of her guides had told her such reenactments took place in some castles throughout the country. "I—sorry to interrupt. I just need to get to my car."

She started to step forward, but the Gorgeous Scot intercepted her, his eyes narrowed. His gaze swept over her from head to toe, taking in her disheveled brown hair and her navy blue maxi dress, and Fiona flushed at his appraisal. His eyes darkened with something she couldn't identify before he met her gaze again.

"Who are ye, lass?" he demanded. "A Sassenach spy? One of Dughall's whores here tae spy on me?"

Fiona gasped, anger coursing through her. Who the hell was this guy—and what was this? If this was a reenactment, he was taking it way too far.

"I don't know what you're talking about, but I was just leaving," she snapped, moving around him, but he again blocked her path.

"Not 'til ye tell us who ye are," the Gorgeous Scot demanded.

"I—I don't have to," she said, pulling herself up to her full height, though she barely reached his broad shoulders. She glared at him. "Now—I don't know what type of reenactment this is, but I'm leaving and you're going to get the hell out of my way!"

"The lass has a mouth on her," said the other handsome Scot, amusement dancing in his eyes.

"'Tis no cause for laughter, Ronan," the Gorgeous Scot grumbled. "If Dughall sent a spy—"

"Let's bring her tae yer father. He can ask—"

"No. If she's a spy, I want tae question her," the Gorgeous Scot's eyes sparked dangerously, and she felt another inappropriate rush of desire.

Fiona swallowed hard. Spy? They thought she was some sort of spy? Her mind clawed through possibilities and reasons—maybe this was an interactive reenactment in which she had to play along. Maybe they were being filmed. She looked around for cameras, but there were none.

"Looking for Dughall's backup, are ye, lass?" demanded the Gorgeous Scot. He stepped forward, and Fiona yelped as he swung her up into his arms, carrying her down the corridor.

"Eadan, what are ye—?" the other man demanded, exasperated.

"I'll get my answers from the lass—alone."

Now, Fiona's fear returned. She was pretty sure that in reenactments—even interactive ones—the actors weren't allowed to touch the participants. She began to struggle in his grip.

"I didn't sign up to be in this, OK? I found this

town by chance. Show's over. I just want to get back to my car."

Eadan gave her a sharp look but kept walking. They went up a series of winding stairs; her struggles were useless against his strength. He kept her in his arms until they entered a massive room—a medieval chamber—that was the size of her one-bedroom apartment back in Chicago.

Fiona stumbled back as soon as he released her. She looked around, terrified. Where were the cameras? The other tourists?

"What are ye looking for, lass?" Eadan demanded. "Ye willnae find any of Dughall's men here to save ye."

"What the hell are you talking about?" Fiona roared. "Who the hell is Dughall? Look—I—I don't know what is going on, but I just want to go back to my car and get back to Inverness."

"Inverness?" he hissed. "What business do ye have in Inverness?"

"I don't want to be a part of this damned reenactment!" Fiona shouted, to whoever could hear. "I just want out!"

"Reenactment?" Eadan's handsome brows knitted together in confusion. "What are ye on about, lass? And what type of gown is this? Ye're almost naked. Even whores doonae put their wares on display like this."

Fiona glared at him. He wasn't going to drop the act. And whoever was holding this reenactment wasn't ending it. Maybe she had to play along in order for it to end? She was certain that keeping a tourist hostage and forcing them to play along with a reenactment they didn't sign up for was illegal, but if that's what it took to get the hell out of this castle—

Fiona stilled, her heart leaping into her throat. *The castle.* When she'd entered its courtyard, it had been in ruins. Now, from what she could tell, and from what she'd seen as Eadan carried her up the stairs, it was fully functional.

Again, her mind struggled to keep up. These men—these actors—must have moved her. It was disturbing—and definitely illegal—but whoever ran this reenactment had to have moved her. Her explanation for all of this was getting more far-fetched, but there was no other explanation.

"Trying tae come up with more lies, lass?" Eadan asked, his eyes narrowed.

"I—I got lost," she stammered.

"Lost?"

"Yes," she said, trying to come up with a lie that was as close to the truth as possible. If she had to play along to get out of this, so be it. "I—I'm not a whore, but a disgraced woman. I was betrothed to an Englishman who betrayed me. I—I fled from him and ended up here. I only hoped to hide in the cellar for a few days before continuing on my way."

"Do ye think I'm a fool?" Eadan spat. "How did ye get in the castle?"

"I—I snuck inside. In the middle of the night.

I'm—I'm sorry," she said hastily. "Now, if you'll just let me be on my way—"

"And where were ye headed?"

"To—to a nunnery. Jenloss Abbey, just east of here," she stammered, reaching for any scrap of medieval history she could think of. That was where disgraced women went in medieval times—she hoped. She'd seen the name of the abbey in one of her maps and prayed it existed in this time. "It's the only place that would take a fallen woman such as me."

For the first time, a look of belief entered Eadan's eyes, and relief filled her. Now that she'd played along with their ridiculous scenario, would they let her go?

"If—if you would be obliged to provide escort," she continued, hoping she sounded authentic. "I'll just be on my way."

Eadan continued to study her, and for a moment she thought he'd acquiesce, but he shook his head. "Not sure I believe ye, lass."

Fiona's heart sank, and panic surged in her chest. They couldn't keep her here against her will; it was kidnapping.

"I've had enough. If I'm not allowed to leave, I'm contacting the authorities as soon as this is all over," she announced to whoever was listening, and started for the door. But Eadan didn't budge.

"I'll let ye leave. One day."

"What do you mean, one day?" she gasped.

"Ye want tae leave, tae head to this . . . nunnery, aye?"

"Yes," Fiona said, through gritted teeth. So he wasn't going to drop the act.

"Then I'll help get ye there. But ye have tae do something for me first."

Fiona stumbled back, her throat dry. He was the sexiest man she'd ever seen, but he was still a stranger, and if this was some type of weird sex thing—

"'Tis not what ye're thinking, lass," Eadan said with exasperation, taking in her panicked expression. "I'll help ye leave . . . if ye pose as my bride."

CHAPTER 5

*T*he woman's lovely brown eyes widened, and her mouth fell open with astonishment. Eadan's heart hammered in his chest as he studied her; the idea had come to him out of nowhere. He'd just realized how much it would help him to have her pose as his bride. Her appearance couldn't have come at a more perfect moment. He'd been trying to think of a way—any way—to postpone or call off the marriage to Magaidh. He needed time to figure out what Dughall and his clan were up to. And now a solution had fallen into his lap, though he wasn't yet certain how his plan would work.

At the first sight of her, rage had filled him at the thought of one of Dughall's spies sneaking into the castle. But something else had also seized him; an unwanted rush of lust. Her long, wavy hair, the color of chestnuts, was tousled about her shoulders, as if she'd just stumbled from bed. Her features were soft and feminine, her mouth full and sensual, her deep brown eyes framed by thick lashes. She wore a gown that left nothing to the imagination; he could see the hard peaks of her nipples straining against its thin fabric.

Eadan gritted his teeth against another surge of desire. Now was not the time to think about bedding the bonnie lass, though he'd been quelling his desire ever since he swung her up into his arms and carried her to his chamber, with her lush curves pressed against his body.

"What—I don't know—no—that's—" she sputtered, pulling him back to the present. "You're insane. This is insane. I'm calling the cops as soon as I leave!"

Her eyes scanned the chamber as she shouted these last words, and he frowned, his suspicions again aroused. Why did she keep looking around? Perhaps she *was* one of Dughall's spies, and he'd already played into her hands.

But something told him this wasn't the case. As soon as she'd spouted that ridiculous story about being a fallen woman and going to a nunnery, he knew she couldn't be a spy. No spy would come up with such a weak story. They'd be more composed, more prepared.

"I'm not marrying you!" she spat. "I just want to get back to my car!"

Eadan frowned. He didn't know of this "car" she kept speaking of, but he could only assume he was missing something through her strange accent, and she meant to say "carriage". His suspicions about her spying for Dughall vanished; her confusion and fluster seemed genuine.

"I ken ye're lying about who ye are, lass, but I doonae care. Ye're not leaving this castle without my help. I just need tae end—or postpone—a betrothal. The best way tae do that is with a bride. I'll say we wed in the past, and we thought it was annulled," he said, thinking aloud. "It'll give me some time, then I'll help ye tae the nunnery—or wherever ye're off tae."

Horror infused her expression, and she pressed her hand to her mouth. Tears filled her eyes, and his heart filled with both sympathy and annoyance. Was the idea of posing as his bride so abominable?

"I doonae wish tae harm ye. Look, lass, I assume ye have no money," he continued, eyeing her thin gown with skepticism. "The village is a ways, and there've been raids by bandits—'tis not safe out there. Even if I tried tae let ye go, my father would want ye held until it's confirmed ye're not a spy—from the English or another clan. Believe it or not, I'm offering ye help."

"I can't stay here," she whispered, her face draining of color. "Please—can you end this reenactment? I won't go to the cops; I want to go home."

"I doonae ken what 'reenactment' ye're speaking of," he said, shaking his head. "Or 'cops.' Ye're an intruder in my castle, but I can help ye. I just need yer help in return."

She remained pale, taking several deep breaths, before meeting his eyes.

"May—may I ask you something?" she asked.

"Aye."

"What—what year is it?"

He studied her, dread coiling around his spine. Perhaps she wasn't right in the head—given her rants and ravings, it would make sense. Perhaps a healer needed to examine her.

She was looking at him with a wild, frightened look, like a rabbit ensnared in a trap. He felt an odd need to comfort her, and reached out to take her hand, and warmth filled him at her touch. He led her to a chair in the corner of the chamber where he sat her down.

"What's yer name?" he asked gently.

"Fiona," she whispered.

Fiona. It was a lovely name; it suited her.

"Fiona," he said, "'tis the year of our Lord, 1390."

"Oh my God," she breathed.

She searched his eyes as if trying to determine his words were true. He evenly held her gaze. Fiona let out a curse that even the most lowborn of his male servants wouldn't use, before her eyes went hazy and she fainted, falling forward into his arms.

"Ye cannae tell me ye think tae keep her here," Ronan said in a terse whisper.

Fiona was now lying in his bed, still asleep from her dead faint. He thought of waking her, but after confirming that she still breathed, he determined that she needed her rest. And he needed to put his plans in motion—if she agreed to pose as his bride.

"Not forever. I need her tae pose as my bride for a brief time, 'til I can figure out what Clan Acheson is up tae."

Ronan looked at him in disbelief.

"Are ye mad, Eadan?" he roared, and Eadan gestured for him to lower his voice. "This betrothal's the only thing that's stopped our clans from—"

"I cannae marry Magaidh. They're planning tae destroy us."

"And what proof do ye have? Is it that ye doonae want tae marry Magaidh? Is this a way of—"

"No," Eadan said, though it was true; he had no desire to marry the cruel Magaidh. "If I thought Dughall's intentions were honorable, I'd marry the lass. Ye ken my duty is tae Clan Macleay and nothing else."

He held Ronan's eyes. Ronan's expression softened, and he heaved a sigh.

"Just give me a few days, Ronan," Eadan continued. "I wouldnae put the clan in danger if I didnae think something was awry. I'm doing this for all of us. I need time. Please."

"Fine," Ronan muttered, after a pause. "But

then ye're marrying Magaidh and letting this poor lass leave."

"Thank ye." His gaze strayed to the beautiful intruder who still lay sprawled on his bed. "Now I just have tae convince her."

Ronan followed his gaze, his mouth tightening.

"What do ye plan tae do? Tell everyone yer bride just happened tae appear? One with strange clothes and an odd tongue?"

"I've a plan," Eadan said, his eyes still on Fiona's sleeping form. He only hoped it would work.

CHAPTER 6

*F*or a few glorious seconds when Fiona awoke, she thought she was back in her room at the bed-and-breakfast in Inverness, and the events of the previous day were just a weird twisted dream. But as she opened her eyes and found that she was in a large bed in a medieval chamber, she wanted to scream. She remembered the Gorgeous Scot—Eadan—telling her, with a straight face and absolute sincerity, that the year was 1390.

She sat up and nearly jumped from her skin at the sight of Eadan at her bedside, seated on a chair. His partially opened tunic revealed a hint of muscular torso, and his dark hair was rumpled, as if he'd raked his hands through it several times. His cerulean blue eyes, filled with caution, studied her as if she were a rabid animal on the verge of attack.

Fiona ignored the surge of desire that flowed through her, taking a breath. She had the horrible feeling that this was no reenactment, and that Eadan spoke the truth. She was somehow, inexplicably in the year 1390.

"Morning, lass," Eadan said, his tone as cautious as his expression. "I take it ye slept well."

"I—I need to leave. Please," she said, stumbling out of bed on shaky legs.

If she was indeed in 1390, she had to figure out how to get back. She'd arrived in the cellar of the castle. Maybe that was where—the portal was? She had to stifle a hysterical laugh at the thought, but if she'd arrived in the fourteenth century, it had been through some sort of portal. Unless she just had a complete breakdown and this entire situation was in her head.

"I doonae think so," Eadan said, getting to his feet. "No one besides myself and my cousin ken ye're here. If ye go wandering about the castle, my father and the other clan nobles will want tae question ye."

Panic flooded her body, and she took several calming breaths. *Don't panic,* she urged herself. *Think.*

"May—may I look out the window?" she asked, speaking past dry lips.

Eadan gave her a puzzled look, but he nodded. She moved past him and peered out the window.

Outside, there were no ruins of a medieval village, her car, or any hint of modernity. Instead, there was a large circular courtyard surrounded on all sides by the castle. Servants in medieval clothing bustled to and fro—a stable boy led two horses toward the gate, two chambermaids carried a large bucket in between them, several male servants carried sacks of what looked like wheat into the side entrance of the castle.

Beyond the courtyard, there was no sign of tourists, cars, cement-paved roads, or any signs of the twenty first century.

Fiona swayed on her feet, clutching the side of the window. Eadan was instantly at her side, helping her back to the chair as he'd done the night before.

To her relief, he said nothing, allowing her to lean forward to press her fingertips to her forehead. Her mind spun, even as she tried to keep calm. *Thirteen ninety.* How was this even possible?

She dimly realized that Eadan was now speaking, and she had to force herself to concentrate on his words.

"I still doonae believe yer story, but I doubt ye're a spy. I do believe ye're eager to leave, and I can help ye with that."

She looked up at him, her heart hammering. "Thank you."

"But the terms havenae changed," he said, holding her gaze. "Ye must help me first."

Dread curled around her spine as she remembered his insane proposition from the night before. A part of her had hoped she hadn't remembered that correctly, that traveling through time had messed with her memory.

"No," she said, at the same time that he said, "I need ye tae pose as my bride."

Fiona glared at him. She was still trying to come to terms with the fact that she might be in another time—and he wanted her to pose as his bride?

"Are you out of your mind?" she demanded. "I'm leaving here, and—"

"I'm giving ye a choice, lass; I willnae force ye tae stay. But if ye try tae leave on yer own, without a penny to yer name, ye'll find it difficult. Someone will stop ye, and bring ye back to me, or to my father, and as I've said before, ye'll have tae deal with stern questions from the other nobles. Tensions are high between our clans, they willnae believe yer story of just happening to arrive here. I'm guessing ye willnae get very far. Or," he continued, his tone softening, "ye can let me help ye. It willnae be a real marriage, just for show, so I can end my betrothal and get tae the bottom of something. If ye help me, I'll help ye get back. Ye have my vow."

Fiona closed her eyes, dazed. When he laid it out like that, it almost seemed rational. *Can you get me six hundred years into the future?* she thought, dazed.

There was still a part of her that clung to the hope of a logical conclusion—that she was dreaming, in some twisted reenactment, or that Eadan, Ronan, and the people in medieval clothing milling around the castle grounds were all crazy.

She needed proof first. Proof that she was indeed in 1390. If so, his proposition was . . . logical. She had no other allies in this time, no other ways of getting out of here. Eadan hadn't harmed her, and he seemed genuine.

"I—I need to confirm something first," she said, trying to keep her voice calm. She didn't want to tell him she was from the future; she had the feeling that wouldn't go over well. She'd have to stick to her made-up-on-the-spot story. "I want you to take me to the nearest village. I—I don't need to talk to anyone. I just need to look around. Please," she said, as he studied her with suspicion. "And then—" Fiona took a breath. She couldn't believe she was saying this, but what choice did she have? "And then I'll pose as your bride."

He relaxed and nodded.

"I'll have tae get ye some clothes," he said, his eyes raking over her, and her face flamed at his critical appraisal. "If anyone stops us, ye're tae say nothing, understand? We'll stay tae the back of the grounds tae avoid being seen."

She nodded, relief flowing through her as he left. As soon as he was gone, she checked every square inch of the room, but there was not a single outlet or hint of anything modern.

Eadan returned more quickly than she'd thought, with a white tunic, an underdress, a green gown, and plaid fabric that she could use as a cloak, something Eadan called an *airisaidh*.

"Had tae tell quite the story tae get those

clothes," he grumbled, before leaving the room to allow her to change.

Fiona looked down at the clothes, nervous. She was used to simple maxi dresses or jeans and button-down shirts. But getting dressed was intuitive, and she slipped into the underdress and tunic before stepping into the green gown. She took special care to wrap the plaid cloak around herself, wanting to be as unobtrusive as possible.

She went to the door and swung it open. Eadan's gaze raked over her, a strange look filling his eyes. Desire? But it was gone before she could interpret it. But that didn't stop her mouth going dry, and a hot spiral of arousal from coiling through her as his eyes locked with hers.

What the hell was wrong with her? She needed to come to terms with this whole time travel thing, not get distracted by the handsome Scot.

"Remember, say nothing," he said. "When we return, we come straight back tae my chamber."

"Agreed."

They took the back entrance out of the castle, and she kept her head bowed low beneath her cloak. He led her out of the the courtyard toward the stables where he fetched a horse from a stable boy who gave her a curious look.

Eadan gently helped her up onto his horse, and she tried not to react to his closeness when he placed his arms around her, holding her close as they rode away from the castle.

Fiona took in their surroundings as they rode,

and her heart sank. They were on a winding dirt road that cut through endless fields of green; there was no sign of modern paved roads, signs, or cars. In the far distance, she could make out manor homes and villages dotting the surrounding lands.

Eadan slowed the horse as they reached the outskirts of a small yet bustling medieval village. Fiona took in the cobblestoned streets, the thatch-roofed cottages, blacksmith and carpenter's shops, and an ale house. The villagers who roamed through the streets and tended to the surrounding fields with horses and plows all wore medieval clothing—long tunics, plain gowns, and breeches.

She could try to convince herself that this was an elaborate reenactment; there were plenty of authentic medieval villages in Scotland. But Fiona took in the faces of the villagers, their expressions ranging from neutral to blank to weary. They weren't playacting. This wasn't some elaborate joke, or reenactment. This was real life. She was in the year 1390.

"Lass," Eadan said, his voice rumbling in her ear. He must have felt the tension in her body. "I assume this isnae where ye meant tae arrive?"

"You can say that," Fiona replied, taking a steadying breath.

He turned the horse and took them back to the castle. Fiona clenched her shaking hands at her sides as a stable boy took the horse from them, and they headed inside the castle through the rear entrance. She was so consumed by her turbulent thoughts that she barely noticed the servant who stopped them.

"Dughall wishes tae speak tae ye, Laird Macleay," he said, his eyes straining toward Fiona with curiosity. At her side, Eadan stiffened.

"I'll be right there."

Eadan gripped her arm, leading her back to his chamber, and she was glad for his firm hand. Her disorientation made it difficult to walk.

Once they arrived in his chamber, he closed the door behind them. Fiona walked to the bed on shaky legs and sank down into it, taking a deep breath.

"I have tae take my leave, but I'll be back shortly," Eadan said. He gestured to a table in the center of the room, where a chambermaid had left a tray of food. "There's food and drink if ye're hungry."

Fiona gave him a brief nod of thanks. Eadan continued to study her. Though his body was tense, his voice remained gentle.

"Have ye decided? Will ye pose as my bride? Or do ye want tae take a chance on yer own?"

Fiona pressed her fingers to her temple. She'd fallen through time to end up in 1390. Thus far, Eadan was her only ally, and potentially the only one who could help her.

"I'll pose as your bride," Fiona whispered.

CHAPTER 7

*E*adan tried not to let the expression on Fiona's face affect him, though she looked as if he'd just sentenced her to death. If he thought her story was false before, he was now certain of it. No one would be this eager to get to a nunnery. Dread, wariness, and fear clouded her face. A surge of protectiveness filled him; what was she running from? Or whom? If he could get her to open up to him; he'd happily help her—but only after he ended his betrothal to Magaidh and figured out what Dughall's true plans were.

"Fiona," he said gently, reaching out to touch her face. She raised her eyes to his, and he noticed with concern that her brown eyes glistened with tears. "Ye only need tae pose as my bride for a brief time, then I'll help get ye tae yer destination."

"What if you can't?" she asked, her voice wavering.

"I'll do everything I can," he promised.

45

Though she still looked uneasy, she gave him a shaky smile. Eadan realized how close they stood together—her natural scent, which smelled of honey and roses, teased his nostrils. Desire flowed through him as his gaze dropped to her full, sensual mouth. And he couldn't help himself—his hands dropped from her face to her waist, and he pressed her close to him before capturing her mouth with his own.

Fiona responded instantly, returning his kiss, and his arousal spiked. He pressed her lush body even closer, plundering her mouth with his. As her hands raised to his neck, gripping his hair, he felt himself harden against his breeches.

His hands tightened around her waist as his tongue probed her mouth, and she moaned. Desire had cast all reason aside. In mere seconds he'd be unable to stop himself from leading her to the bed, to peppering the lovely arch of her throat with kisses, to—

The sound of Ronan clearing his throat brought him back to the present, and he abruptly released Fiona, who looked flustered and out of breath. Fiona lowered her eyes, a lovely blush staining her cheeks.

Eadan whirled to face Ronan, more irritated than he knew he should be, especially when he saw the glint of amusement in his cousin's eyes.

"Sorry tae interrupt," Ronan said, not looking sorry at all. He gestured for Eadan to approach.

Eadan did so reluctantly, his senses still on fire after his kiss with Fiona. Ronan lowered his voice.

"Did the lass agree tae yer plan?"

"Aye," Eadan said.

"Wonder how ye convinced her," Ronan said, his mouth twitching.

"What did ye come here tae tell me?" Eadan asked, irritated.

"I found a man willing tae help with yer story. Had tae pay him a decent amount of coin," Ronan said, with a trace of annoyance.

Relief filled Eadan, and his annoyance with his cousin faded. Ronan was unflinchingly loyal and Eadan trusted him more than anyone.

He straightened, glancing back at Fiona. She still looked flustered by their kiss—her breathing was still rapid, her face flushed. He forced himself to not let his gaze linger on the fullness of her lips, or the curve of her breasts against her bodice. He shouldn't have kissed the tempting lass—he needed to focus.

"I've a plan," he told her. "But ye'll have tae play yer part. Are ye willing?"

Fiona swallowed and gave him a quick nod.

"I'll have to be," she said. "Tell me what to do."

EADAN STOOD in the center of the great hall, facing the nobles of his clan, hoping that his expression was appropriately sincere—and contrite. He'd just told them quite the tale; he could only hope they believed his story.

They all looked at him in astonishment and disbelief. Confusion filled his father's expression, while Dughall, Eadan noted with unease, studied him with suspicion.

"Ye mean tae tell us ye're already married?" his father demanded. "And ye never thought tae mention this before the betrothal?"

"I thought it was annulled. 'Twas a foolish thing tae do; my shame is why I never told anyone," Eadan said, trying to school his expression to one of shame. "Never thought I'd see her again."

Out of the corner of his eye, he saw Ronan's mouth twitch, though he'd dutifully remained stone-faced as Eadan told his tale.

Eadan was rather proud of the story he'd invented. He'd told them that he'd traveled to England two years prior—which he had. But the next part was pure invention.

During his time there, he'd stopped at a small isolated town on the Welsh border where he'd met Fiona. They'd fallen in love and foolishly—impetuously—gotten married by a local priest. But they'd realized the error of their impulsiveness and went their separate ways before they consummated the marriage, thus rendering it invalid. The only person he'd told was Ronan; he was ashamed of doing something so foolish and out of character.

Fiona had arrived at the castle last night. Her husband-to-be had cast her aside after discovering her marriage to Eadan was still valid, as the priest who married them logged it in the church records and never removed it.

With no family and nowhere to turn, Fiona had come here for Eadan's help; the priest refused to annul the marriage at just her request; he wanted Eadan's request as well. Fiona, he insisted, was on her way to Jenloss Abbey; she had no intention of interfering with his betrothal to Magaidh. She just wanted the annulment and then she'd be on her way.

"I've already sent a messenger with my request tae the priest," Eadan said, exchanging a brief look with Ronan. The man Ronan had hired would pose as this messenger; he'd agreed to tell the nobles he dispatched the message if they asked. "But it may take time tae get confirmation the priest has removed the marriage from record," Eadan continued. "'Til then, the betrothal will have tae be put on hold."

"'Tis convenient, this lass showing up as ye're about to marry and end the feud between our clans," said Dughall, his eyes narrowed. "How do we ken she's not some spy, here tae end our truce?"

"That's what I thought as well. I assure ye, I've questioned her, and she's no spy. Just a frightened lass with no place tae go," Eadan said. He turned to his father. "Clan Macleay is all about honor—and duty. While I'm married tae the lass, I'm honor bound tae help her."

"Aye," his father said, after a long pause. "But

I'm disappointed in ye, son. What was it about the lass that made ye marry her?"

"'Twas lust, I'm ashamed to say," he said. "My former bride is a beauty—nothing close tae Maga-idh," he added hastily, looking at Dughall, who scowled. That was the hardest part of his elaborate lie. Fiona made his loins stir while Magaidh left him cold. "I wasnae thinking with my head, Father."

"We can all understand that, aye?" Ronan added. Eadan was grateful for Ronan's presence here, he'd played along well. "Seen a lass we cannae get enough of?"

Everyone except Dughall nodded, some chuckling with amusement.

"I want tae see the lass. Yer Sassenach wife," Dughall said, glowering at him.

Eadan nodded; he'd been expecting this, though his heart filled with dread. He and Ronan had prepared Fiona the best they could for questioning, but this was where everything could fall apart.

"She's resting, but when she's—" he began, hoping this would dissuade him.

"No. I want tae see the lass for myself. Hear her version of the story."

Dughall's hard gaze remained on him, and Eadan's stomach tightened. He nodded and turned to Ronan, who had also gone tense. Ronan left the hall and after several moments returned with Fiona.

He could tell she was terrified; her hands shook slightly at her sides, and her skin had paled, but she held her head high as she entered the room.

Eadan turned to face the nobles. A rush of jealousy coursed through him as one of the nobles, McFadden, eyed her with lustful appreciation.

"I see why ye married 'er, Macleay," he said.

"She's still my wife, McFadden," Eadan growled. "'Til it's annulled, ye'll treat her with respect."

"Fiona," Eadan's father interjected, giving McFadden a look of warning, before turning his focus to Fiona, "tell us how ye've come tae us."

"My—my betrothed cast me aside when he found out about my marriage," Fiona said, her voice trembling.

"Yer accent is strange, lass," Dughall said, his eyes narrowed with suspicion.

"I—I traveled a great deal when I was a child," Fiona stammered. "My father was a traveling merchant before he became a farmer; he took me and my mother with him on his travels. I picked up many foreign tongues."

"And where is yer family now?" Dughall pressed.

"I've no family. They all died of the plague years ago. I used my last coin traveling here; I hoped that Eadan would help me get the annulment and send me to Jenloss Abbey where I wish to spend the rest of my days. Please," her voice cracked, and a tear spilled from her eyes, one that he suspected was genuine. "I—I don't know how I've come to be in this ti—situation, and I just want to go back to my own—to a home."

She pressed her hands to her mouth, closing her eyes, tears streaming from beneath her lids.

Eadan was at her side at once, pulling her into the circle of his arms. She buried her face into his neck, and he held her close, unable to stop himself from pressing his lips to her hair, whispering words of comfort. Her despair was no act, and for a moment, Eadan forgot about all the eyes on them. He wanted nothing more than to take her pain away.

"Nothing more needs tae be said," his father said, getting to his feet, leaning on his cane. His expression had softened, and he studied Fiona with sympathy. "My son is honor bound tae the lass while she's his wife. The betrothal's on hold 'til his marriage is annulled and we send her on her way."

CHAPTER 8

*W*hen Eadan first told Fiona his plan, she'd thought it was crazy, but he'd asked her to trust him. He told her they would most likely want to question her, and she'd tried to remain calm as she waited outside the hall while Eadan addressed the nobles.

Eadan's kiss had thoroughly disoriented her; on top of that, she had to convince a group of fourteenth-century Highlanders that she was a fallen English woman in need of a home. She'd always been a terrible liar, but she was determined to wing it. She needed Eadan as an ally in this time; he seemed to be her only way of getting back.

When she'd entered the room filled with the nobles of two clans—people who'd been dead for centuries in her time, she'd fought to keep her bearings. But she stuck to her tactic of sticking as close to the truth as possible, and as the craziness of her circumstances hit her; the tears had been real. She didn't need to pretend that she was scared and overwhelmed. She had no idea how she'd gotten to be in 1390 and "married" to a Highland laird—however gorgeous he was. She just wanted to get back to her own time.

Most of the nobles seemed to believe her story, and she saw relief in Eadan's blue eyes as he escorted her from the hall. A ripple of electricity flowed through her at his nearness, and she forced herself to step out of his grasp. A brief flash of something—perhaps hurt—flashed in Eadan's eyes, and he dropped his hands to his side as she followed him down the corridor and up a winding set of stairs.

When they reached the top landing, he glanced around to make certain they were alone, before lowering his voice.

"Ye did well," Eadan said. His tone softened, as he continued, "And I meant what I said—I'll help ye get tae wherever ye need tae go once this is all over."

His eyes were sincere, and she relaxed. It wasn't like he wasn't offering to help her for nothing in return, but a rush of gratitude still coursed through her, though she had no idea how he'd help her get back to the present.

Eadan turned, continuing down the hall until they reached a large chamber at the far end. Inside, an elderly woman with gray-streaked, blond hair and kind eyes stood. From her plain gown and apron, Fiona guessed she was a servant. The woman gave Fiona a warm smile.

"This is Una. She'll help ye get settled and show ye around the castle. I'll come by tae collect ye before supper," he said, holding her gaze, and she understood his meaning. Eadan would need to prep her before she sat down for a meal with the other guests.

Eadan left them alone, and Fiona looked around. The chamber seemed even larger than Eadan's, complete with a fireplace, a large arched window through which sunlight filtered in, and a massive curtained bed in the center. It was way too big of a room for just her.

"Ye're wife of the laird," Una said, as if reading her mind, giving her a warm smile. "Tis your home while ye're here."

"For now," Fiona said hastily.

"No one would be bothered if ye stayed, m'lady," Una said, moving over to the large bed, where a gown lay. "Magaidh is a devil in a lass's body. She hates the laird, everyone can see it. I'm a feared she'll kill him in his sleep."

Fiona blinked, surprised that Una was being so open with her, a virtual stranger.

"But ye're different, I can already tell. There's a kindness tae ye, and ye're quite bonnie. I can see why the laird fell for ye. It's my hope that the laird keeps ye here."

Fiona shook her head; she needed to make it clear she had no intention of staying.

"I—I have every intention of going to the nunnery," Fiona said. "I've no plans to interfere with his betrothal."

Una pressed her lips together but nodded, turning her focus to the gown on the bed.

"The gown ye're wearing isnae suitable for the wife of the laird. I'll help ye get dressed, and then—"

"That's not necessary," Fiona said. She already found having a dedicated servant odd—it would be even weirder to have someone help her get dressed.

Una studied her, surprised, before her lips curved into a smile.

"When Magaidh comes tae visit, she insists on having three chambermaids tae help her dress," she said, shaking her head. "I suppose ye're different. I'll be waiting in the hall while ye dress. When ye're ready, I can show ye around the castle."

Fiona sighed. She had no desire to get into a rivalry with this Magaidh woman, but Una already seemed to like her more. It might be harder to stay out of the Eadan-Magaidh betrothal drama than she'd thought.

Una left the room, and Fiona got dressed, her hands trembling as she slipped on the underdress, then the tunic, and then the gown, which was deep blue and made of a finer fabric than the one she previously wore.

As she dressed, her mind whirled. The events of the day had flown by with such swiftness she'd barely had time to process it all. Now, the biggest question of all loomed in her mind—how had she come here? She recalled the rush of wind—and that woman. The same woman she'd seen in the museum, and at the ruins of the castle. That woman had something to do with her time travel, she was certain of it.

Fiona expelled a breath. If she went back to the cellar, she could see if the portal was still there. Una's tour of the castle couldn't have come at a better time.

After she'd dressed, Una looked her over, giving her a nod of approval before showing her around the castle, pointing out the upstairs chambers, then the great hall, the kitchens, and the inner court-yard. As they walked, the servants they passed studied her with curious gazes; she suspected the news of her arrival had already swept over the castle.

Once Una led her to the outer courtyard, pointing out the nearby stables, it truly hit her—she was in an actual thriving fourteenth-century castle. For the first time since she'd arrived, she allowed a sense of awe to sweep over her as she took in her surroundings. Macleay Castle was made of gray stone, its turreted towers winding toward the clear blue sky, surrounded by lush forests, overlooking a nearby lake. The castle could have been on a post-card for Scotland in her own time.

My own time, Fiona thought, reality seizing her by the throat. She needed to find a way to get back to her own time. She realized that Una hadn't shown her the lower part of the castle—the cellar, where she'd arrived.

"If you don't mind, I'd like to walk around a bit. Just—to clear my head. A lot has happened," she said, as Una started to lead her back to her chamber.

"Of course, m'lady. Ye can find me in the kitchens if ye need anything."

Fiona turned, pretending to head back to the courtyard. Once Una was out of sight, she turned, making her way down the long corridor past the great hall, reaching the stairwell that led to the cellar.

She paused, listening, but heard no one below. She descended the stairs, lifting up her skirts to avoid tripping.

Her heart slammed against her ribcage as she stepped inside the cellar, looking around.

But . . . it was an ordinary cellar. Just filled with stores of herbs, spices, and barrels of wine and ale. No vortex of wind. No strange woman. No telltale sign of anything odd or supernatural.

I'm trapped. A surge of frustration paired with fear filled her, and she leaned back against the wall, closing her eyes. She stilled when she heard voices from above, just as she'd heard the night she arrived.

"And is she staying in yer bed, then?"

"No, Magaidh. Of course not."

It was Eadan—Eadan and that woman he was betrothed to, Magaidh. She knew she shouldn't eavesdrop, but something compelled her to the base of the stairs where she listened intently.

"Our marriage was never consummated. I'm only showing her kindness now. She means nothing tae me—I've every intention of wedding ye."

"My father said she's bonnie. Are ye certain ye're not using her tae end our betrothal?"

There was a hint of warning in Magaidh's seductive tone.

"No," he said fiercely. From where she stood, Fiona could see their shadows move. She suspected Eadan was touching her cheek, and an inappropriate rush of jealousy flowed through her. "I—" His voice wavered, as if he were forcing himself to continue— "I wish to marry ye."

"Good," Magaidh said, satisfaction shaping her words.

Fiona held herself still as their footfalls disappeared, pushing aside her jealousy. What Eadan said—or did—with Magaidh was none of her concern. She was only posing as his bride until she could figure out how to get the hell out of 1390 and back to her own time. And that was what she would do. *Somehow.*

CHAPTER 9

*W*hen Eadan came to her chamber to collect her for supper, he seemed to detect something was wrong.

"Are ye all right, lass?" he asked, his blue eyes sweeping over her face.

"I'm fine," Fiona said, trying to keep her tone neutral. She resisted the urge to ask about his moment in the corridor with Magaidh, reminding herself that it was none of her concern.

His eyes told her he didn't believe her, but he changed topics, giving her a brief overview of what to say in case anyone asked too many questions.

"The guests will stare, and there will be gossip; try yer best tae ignore it," Eadan continued. "My hope is that most of the questions will be directed tae me."

"Maybe I can take my meals in my rooms," Fiona said, uneasy at the thought of facing other people in this time. "If people are going to ask too many—"

"It'll seem more suspicious if I hide ye away in your chamber," Eadan said, shaking his head. "Ye willnae be here long, lass, and then they'll be on tae the next piece of gossip."

Fiona nodded, taking a deep breath to quell her hammering heartbeat. She told herself that this was just a meal; she'd already done the hard part and told the nobles her story, which they seemed to buy, so this should be a piece of cake.

Still, her throat went dry with anxiety as Eadan escorted her from her chamber and down to the great hall.

Eadan was right about the stares. As soon as they stepped into the hall, all eyes turned to her. Fiona swallowed, averting her eyes from the guests as Eadan gestured for her to take a seat several seats away from him. For appearance's sake, he couldn't have the "wife" he was on the verge of sending away seated at his side.

As the meal began, she tried to ignore the probing stares of the guests, focusing only on her meal and the surroundings. The hall was massive, and there must have been at least fifty guests. She, Eadan, and the nobles sat at the head table, while several other tables were situated around the hall for the other guests. Two large fireplaces situated at opposite ends of the hall, along with multiple candles provided ample illumination for the large space.

Fiona turned her focus to the food. To her surprise, she found it delicious. The guests were served roasted chicken, bread, and assorted vegetables with wine or ale. From what scant medieval history she knew, she'd assumed the food would be bland without the modern day spices she was used to. Instead, everything was earthier, hitting her tongue with an array of flavors.

She was halfway through eating her meal when a woman who sat opposite her spoke up.

"Ye're from England, are ye?" the woman asked. "Yer accent is not the same as the English."

Fiona looked up. The woman had pointed, hawk-like features, with dark eyes and inky black hair. She surveyed Fiona with cool eyes.

Fiona took a breath and repeated the story she'd told the nobles about her travels as a child, picking up foreign tongues which influenced her accent. But the woman's cool expression remained, and dread pooled in her stomach. She prayed she wouldn't ask any more questions.

"I'm called Elspeth Graeme," she said, her tone cool. "I'd love tae get tae ken ye more, before ye're on yer way. My home isnae far from the castle. Ye should stop by for a visit."

Fiona froze, fear filling her at the thought of leaving the castle. Instinctively, her eyes darted to Eadan, but he was engrossed in conversation with Ronan. Would it make her more—or less—suspicious if she refused?

"That would be lovely," Fiona said, with a forced smile. "I will have to ask Eadan, of course."

"Eadan will approve; he was friends with my late husband."

Elspeth stated this in a matter-of-fact way; no sorrow behind her words. Fiona had to hide her astonishment; she seemed far too young to be a widow. She looked to be no older than twenty-three or twenty-four. But then again, people got married younger—and died sooner—here than in her own time.

"I just want tae ken more about the woman Eadan married," Elspeth continued, and Fiona didn't miss the vague suspicion in her voice. "'Tis not like him tae be so impulsive; the whole castle is talking about it."

"It was a foolish thing to do," Fiona said. "I just wish to have our marriage annulled and continue on my way. I've no wish to interfere with his betrothal."

She had the feeling she'd have to repeat this statement many times to get this point across. Elspeth looked pleased by this statement, and Fiona wondered if she was a friend of Magaidh's. Whomever she was, Fiona didn't trust her one bit—there was something disingenuous about her. She hoped that Eadan could get her out of this social call.

Thankfully, the meal ended with no more probing questions from Elspeth or any other guest, and Eadan escorted her back to her chamber. She told him of Elspeth's request, expecting him to tell her he'd get her out of it. Instead, eagerness filled his eyes.

"She's a member of Clan Macleay because of her late husband. But she's close with Magaidh and many nobles of Dughall's clan," he said. "It may be wise for ye tae become friendly with her. While ye're there, perhaps ye'll gain some information about Dughall."

"I don't think we're going to become friendly," Fiona said, recalling Elspeth's coldness.

"Magaidh hates this arrangement as much as I do. I'm sure she's confided in Elspeth about it," Eadan said, waving away her concerns.

"Eadan—I agreed to pose as your bride. I'm no spy. It was difficult enough for me to answer the one question she asked," Fiona protested.

Eadan looked down at her, his expression softening.

"Ye're right. I can only imagine how difficult this has been for ye, but ye've done well. Ye doonae have tae ask her anything, but I do think ye should make an effort tae be friendly. Refusing her invitation only arouses suspicion. Make one brief visit and that should satisfy her."

This didn't make Fiona feel any better. Who knew what type of questions she would ask? But she was pulled from her troubled thoughts when she realized that Eadan wasn't leading her down the familiar corridor that led to her chamber;

instead, he was walking toward the rear of the castle.

"Where are you going?"

"Tis a lovely night," he said, glancing down at her. "I thought ye might want tae enjoy the night air after the day ye've had."

He smiled at her, his blue eyes twinkling, and a rush of heat filled Fiona; for a moment, she forgot all about Elspeth and her clear dislike.

They made their way out the rear of the castle to the inner courtyard. Outside, the air was damp with the promise of rain. He led her to the outer courtyard, taking her just past the gate.

Here, she could see the surrounding landscape, and Fiona let out a soft gasp. Stars blanketed the night sky and moonlight bathed the trees and the nearby lake in an almost ethereal glow. She itched for her sketch pad, wanting nothing more than to commit this image to memory.

"I used to paint," she said, the confession spilling from her lips before she could stop it. "Landscapes just like this. I'd love to paint something like this."

"Aye?" Eadan said, looking at her in surprise. "I've never met a lass who had an interest in painting."

Fiona bit her lip, wondering if she'd said too much. As far as she knew, women weren't allowed to be artists in this time. But Eadan didn't look angry—he looked intrigued.

"A—a friend of my father's was a painter," she

hedged. "He'd sometimes let me paint. I enjoyed it. It helped relax me."

"Perhaps I can get ye some materials. Parchment and pigments," Eadan said, surprising her. "Can be a way of passing the time while ye're here."

"I'd like that," Fiona said, pleasantly surprised.

Eadan smiled, and another rush of warmth swept over her. He was distractingly handsome, and his smile only enhanced his masculine beauty. Unbidden, the memory of his lips on hers sprang into her mind, and she took a breath, forcing her attention back to the surrounding landscape.

"My father used tae take me riding at night, just so we could look out on the lands," Eadan said, following her gaze. "Reminded me of my responsibility tae these lands. Reminded me that one day, it would all be mine."

Fiona studied him, noticing the strain in his eyes. His need to have a complete stranger pose as his bride showed how desperate he must be to protect his clan, and her heart tightened with sympathy.

"I hope you find the information you need," she said. "And who knows? Maybe Elspeth will warm up to me."

"Ye've a kind heart, lass," he said, after a brief pause. He studied her, so intently that she felt her cheeks warm as he appraised her. "And . . . ye can tell me where ye're truly from."

Fiona blinked in astonishment. Eadan was perceptive; he must have sensed that her made-up back story was bull. His eyes probed hers as if willing her to tell the truth, but how could she? How could she tell him she was from the twenty-first century and she'd inexplicably ended up in this time? He would think she was crazy, or even worse, she realized with a shudder, that she was a witch. The fourteenth century wasn't exactly known for forward thinking.

So she averted her gaze, again focusing on the surrounding landscape.

"I'm telling the truth. I—I just want to get to Jenloss Abbey."

Out of the corner of her eye, she saw Eadan stiffen.

"Let's get ye back to yer chamber," he said, and she knew that the brief moment of intimacy they'd just shared had vanished.

CHAPTER 10

*E*adan didn't know how much longer he could stand Dughall's presence. He'd clenched his teeth so many times he feared he'd bite off his own tongue.

It was early the next morning. Eadan, Dughall and their men were out on a hunting trip in the forests that lay just beyond the castle grounds. He'd arranged for the outing before Fiona's mysterious appearance. When he planned the outing, it was with the hope that Dughall would slip and reveal some hint of what he was up to.

But Dughall treated Eadan with barely contained hostility; the postponement of the betrothal and Fiona's abrupt appearance must have angered him. He'd been short and brusque with Eadan and his men all morning, and it was trying Eadan's patience. Any time Eadan attempted to discuss the truce between their clans and what that would entail, Dughall would interrupt and insist they not talk clan business during their leisure time.

Now, he glared at the back of Dughall's balding head as he trudged ahead with his men, scouring the forest for the deer, hares, or wild boars that roamed here. Eadan knew Dughall wouldn't take his "marriage" to Fiona lightly, but he had to admit to himself it wasn't Dughall that bothered him. It was the knowledge that Fiona was lying to him about who she truly was. He had a good instinct about people lying to him. After he'd opened up to her last night, there was a part of him that hoped she'd do the same.

He recalled the way she looked last night in the moonlight; the awe in her lovely brown eyes as she took in the landscape, her full lips slightly parted, her breasts straining against the bodice of her dress . . .

"If ye expect him tae tell ye his dastardly plan, 'tis not working," Ronan said in a low voice, pulling Eadan from his lust-filled reverie. He walked closely at Eadan's side, his gaze trained on Dughall.

"Aye, I ken," Eadan grumbled. "But I had tae try."

Up ahead, Dughall stilled, gesturing for quiet. A deer grazed a clearing up ahead. The men all went still as Dughall steadied his bow, aiming for the deer's flank. He landed the kill, and the deer slumped over on its side.

"Another kill," Dughall said, turning to face Eadan with triumph. "Ye need tae catch up, Eadan.

The chief of Clan Macleay needs tae be a strong hunter. Shows what a good fighter he is. And I want my Magaidh tae have a husband who protects her."

Eadan straightened; this was the direction he'd hoped the conversation would go.

"Aye," Eadan said, moving forward until he was at Dughall's side. "But I fear this business with Fiona could take time tae sort out. Getting an annulment tae a foreign bride is more complicated than I thought. It may be hard tae find the priest who married us."

He watched Dughall carefully, noting the brief flare of rage in his green eyes before it vanished. Dughall smiled, though his face remained tight.

"Ye're an honorable man, Eadan," he said. "I trust ye'll honor yer word tae my daughter once ye've secured yer annulment."

"'Tis a shame yer wife's going tae Jenloss Abbey," said Uisdean, one of Dughall's men, shaking his head. "A bonnie lass with a body like that's not made for life in a nunnery. If she needs someone, I've a vacant spot in my bed for—"

Eadan reacted without thinking. In an instant, he had the man slammed against a tree, his hand around his throat. It wasn't until Ronan's shouts permeated his haze of furor that he realized he was cutting off Uisdean's air.

He released him, stumbling back as Dughall and another one of his men hurried forward, helping Uisdean away from the tree.

"What's gotten intae ye, Eadan?" Dughall roared.

Eadan blinked, his fists clenched at his sides, taking several breaths to calm himself. Hot fury had filled every part of him when Uisdean spoke of Fiona in his bed.

Dughall and his men glared at him, and Eadan cursed himself. He should have restrained himself. This was not the way to get Dughall to open up to him.

"Were ye trying tae kill my man?"

"I'm—sorry," Eadan ground out. "Fiona's still my wife. I willnae have her spoken of like a whore."

"A wife no one kent of 'til the other day. A wife ye supposedly no longer care for," Dughall said, his eyes filling with suspicion.

"I would've reacted the same way had he insulted Magaidh," Eadan lied. "Ye just said I'm a man of honor. Ye ken this tae be true, Dughall."

Dughall didn't reply, his features strained as he glared at Eadan.

"I think we're done hunting for the day," he said tightly.

As they made their way back to the castle, Ronan shot him a look of disbelief. Frustration coursed through him—what was he thinking? But just the thought of what Uisdean had said about Fiona caused another wave of fury to sweep over him.

He offered Uisdean some ale or a meal in the castle after offering another apology, but he stiffly refused, and Dughall and his men left under a haze of tension.

"Eadan—" Ronan began, as soon as the men were gone, and he accompanied him down the long corridor toward his chamber.

"I ken what I did was foolish," Eadan said, as they entered his chamber. "I doonae need ye tae remind me."

Ronan fell silent, studying him closely. "Are ye sure yer—arrangement—with Fiona is a way of holding off the betrothal?"

"Aye. Of course," Eadan said, glaring at him. "Ye ken I've been thinking of ways tae get out of the betrothal for some time now. There's nothing more between me and Fiona, I was just protecting her honor."

Eadan didn't know if he was trying to convince himself or Ronan, but Ronan didn't look convinced by his words.

"Just remember what yer goals are—and killing one of Dughall's men isnae the way tae accomplish 'em."

Ronan left him alone before he could reply. Eadan changed out of his hunting clothes before heading to his private study, where he tried to concentrate on the concerns of the day, looking over a stack of deeds and rents owed that he needed to review. But he found it hard to concentrate, his frustration over his actions during the hunt continuing to plague him.

He didn't look up when he heard a soft knock

on the door, but he stilled when Fiona's familiar sweet scent filled the room. He looked up to find her hovering by the doorway. She looked lovely in a gown of deep crimson paired with a plaid cloak, but her eyes were troubled.

Forgetting his own concerns, he got to his feet and strode to her, a wave of protectiveness sweeping over him.

"Fiona? What is it?"

"I'm more nervous than I expected," she said, giving him a shaky smile, "about my meeting with Elspeth. The carriage is waiting downstairs, but I don't want to leave. I—I've felt safe at the castle for the past couple of days."

"Then ye doonae have tae go," he said swiftly. "I'll say ye've fallen ill, make my excuses."

Fiona's eyes widened in surprise at his concession, and guilt filled him. Had he been so rigid? Did she think she had no choice in the matter?

"No," she said, after a brief pause. "I'll go. I'm sure she'd just reschedule the meeting, and you were right—if I don't go it'll just raise more suspicion. I'll just get this over with. I'm—I'm sorry to have bothered you," she said, looking embarrassed.

"Ye didnae bother me," he insisted. He reached for her hand, and tendrils of heat roiled through him at the contact with her skin. "Ye're helping me, Fiona. And for that I'm grateful."

As her eyes locked with his, the heat that had filled him at her touch ignited into the hot flames of desire. An ache he didn't realize he had until now swelled, and he leaned forward, capturing her lips with his.

She responded, and his erection swelled against his kilt as he pulled her close, reveling in the sensation of her breasts pressed against his chest. He plundered her mouth with his, wanting nothing more than to lower her bodice and seize one of her lovely breasts with his mouth, to lift the hem of her gown to taste the sweetness between her legs, before sinking into her, claiming her body for his own.

But he forced himself to end the kiss and step back, averting his eyes from her flushed face, her parted lips, her desire-laced eyes.

He closed his eyes, turning away from her, reminding himself what was at stake. He'd already angered Dughall by attacking his man, and now he was on the verge of making love to the lass who was only supposed to pose as his wife.

"I—I'm sorry," he said, his voice strained and gruff, "I shouldnae have—"

"It's all right," Fiona whispered. He looked at her, not missing the brief look of hurt in her eyes, before she turned to the door. "I—I need to be on my way."

CHAPTER 11

*E*lectricity buzzed through Fiona at the memory of Eadan's kiss, and she touched her lips as the carriage clattered away from the castle. She'd forgotten all about her nervousness about her visit with Elspeth; instead, all she could think about was Eadan—his masculine scent of spice and rosewood, his tall, muscular body pressed against hers. She'd wanted him to strip her bare and make love to her, and disappointment had roiled through her when he'd stopped.

Fiona expelled a breath, forcing herself back to the present. *It's a good thing he stopped*, she told herself. Yes, he was the most gorgeous man she'd ever seen, and she was undeniably, wildly attracted to him. But there was one glaring problem—he was from a different time, and she needed to focus on getting back to her own time, not on getting laid by the sexy Highlander she was fake married to.

She wanted to laugh at the irony of the only

man she had explosive chemistry with living hundreds of years before she was even born. With Derek there had been no spark, no fire. With Eadan, his touch was akin to a flame that lit up her insides, searing every part of her.

She had to set her tumultuous thoughts aside when the carriage pulled up to a sprawling manor house. She needed to focus, to convince Elspeth that she was no threat, merely a fallen woman who just wanted to be on her way. *Despite the fact that you just kissed Eadan*, a telltale voice whispered in the back of her mind.

A servant opened her carriage door, helping her down. Fiona took another steadying breath. *You can do this, Fiona.* All she knew about the woman, from a brief discussion with Eadan, was that she was a gossip, she was friendly with Magaidh, and she and her late husband's marriage was more of a clan arrangement than anything else. Fiona suspected she was the fourteenth-century equivalent of a rich, bored housewife, and Fiona was an easy target to assuage her boredom. Fiona would just have to be careful not to give her any ammunition for gossip.

A servant led her into the home, down a long ornate hallway, and into a drawing room. Fiona froze when she saw that Elspeth was not alone. Another woman sat opposite her, a beautiful redhead who gave her a look that shone with hostility.

Dread coiled in Fiona's chest; she'd never seen Magaidh, but she had no doubt that this was her.

"Did I not mention Magaidh would join us?" Elspeth asked, her eyes wide in faux apology, though she looked pleased at Fiona's obvious discomfort.

"No," Fiona said tightly, though she forced a smile. "You didn't."

"Fiona," Magaidh said, getting to her feet to approach Fiona. Though she was smiling, her eyes remained cold. "I'm Magaidh of Clan Acheson; Eadan's betrothed."

"Pleased to make your acquaintance," Fiona said stiffly. "I want you to know, I have no intention—"

"Ye've no intention of interfering with the betrothal. Aye, I heard," Magaidh said, though she didn't look convinced. "Yer secret marriage to my Eadan is quite the story among our two clans. I've kent Eadan since he was a lad. He doesnae have a rash bone in his body."

"We both know it was a mistake," Fiona said, hoping that she looked contrite, though she bristled at the way Magaidh referred to Eadan as hers. "I only wish to live a quiet and pious life in the nunnery. I'm grateful that Eadan is helping me."

Magaidh said nothing for a moment, cocking her head to the side as she studied Fiona.

"What is the name of the village ye're from?"

"Kington," Fiona said, trying to keep her voice steady. She'd happened to see the name of the village in a travel brochure she'd flipped through in her own time and told Eadan that was where she was from. She assumed it existed in this century; Eadan hadn't looked suspicious at the name.

"I've never been tae England. But even the Sassenach who come tae visit doonae have an accent such as ye," Magaidh said, studying her with suspicion.

Fiona clenched her hands at her sides. She needed to change the subject, stat. It was all too easy to poke holes in her story. But before she could speak, Magaidh continued, "My Eadan is the most handsome man in the castle, doonae ye agree?"

This was a trap, and Fiona wasn't going to fall for it.

"I thought him handsome once, but I—"

"Elspeth told me how ye were looking at him during supper last night," Magaidh interrupted, with a lethal look in her eyes. She took another step forward and reached out to take Fiona's arm in a bruising grip. Fiona winced. Magaidh's grip wasn't gentle, it would probably leave a bruise.

"I doonae ken what ye're planning, but Eadan belongs tae me. Ye may be staying in his castle, but it's me he'll marry. We all ken ye're a lying whore. Ye're here for Eadan, and I willnae have it," Magaidh hissed.

Fiona struggled to release herself from Magaidh's grasp. This had already gone way worse than she'd expected. Jealousy filled Magaidh's green eyes, which baffled Fiona. Eadan had told her

Magaidh hated this arrangement as much as he did. But it didn't look like this was the case; Magaidh seemed genuinely possessive of Eadan.

A hot rush of defiant anger flowed through Fiona as Magaidh's grip tightened. She didn't know if it was her own jealousy at the possessive way Magaidh referred to Eadan, or her frustration over being dragged into the center of all this, but she couldn't stop her next words.

"You listen to me," she snapped. "I'll not stand for threats from you, or anyone. Now let go of me before you see what I'm capable of."

Both Magaidh and Elspeth blinked in surprise, and Magaidh released her.

"I'll see myself out," she said, pleased at the astonishment in their eyes. Giving them one last defiant glare, Fiona turned to stalk out of the room. But as the rush faded, she realized that she'd officially made two enemies in this time.

WHEN SHE RETURNED to the castle, Fiona was still rattled from her encounter. She'd just have to stay out of Magaidh and Elspeth's crosshairs until she could get out of here.

She was making her way down the corridor to her chamber when she noticed Eadan's father Bran hobbling on his cane in the opposite direction. He moved with great difficulty, taking in great gasps of air.

Fiona hurried to his side.

"Can I help you get somewhere?"

"Aye," Bran said, an embarrassed look crossing his face. "I gave my manservant the afternoon off. Thought I'd be able tae get tae my private study on my own. I'm not a young strong lad anymore."

Fiona took his arm, and he leaned on her as they made their way down the corridor toward his study.

"How are ye finding everything, lass?"

"Lovely. Everyone's been so kind," she lied. There was no need to tell him about the Magaidh-Elspeth drama. "Thank you for letting me stay here. I hope I'm not causing too much trouble."

"My son is a man of honor—he wouldnae turn ye away, nor would I. We'll get yer annulment and send ye on yer way."

Send me to where? Fiona wondered. If she couldn't get back to her own time in the cellar where she'd arrived, she had no idea where another portal was.

She led him into his study, helping him to his chair. Bran's gaze strayed past her, and she turned to follow his gaze. He studied a portrait of a beautiful woman with dark hair and blue eyes. Eadan was the spitting image of her.

"Eadan doted on his mother, and she on him," Bran said, his eyes still on the portrait.

"She was beautiful."

"Aye. Indeed," Bran said, a look of wistfulness paired with grief crossing his face. Fiona turned to leave, but Bran placed his hand on hers. "Eadan marrying ye in secret shocked us all. But a part of me was relieved."

"Relieved?" Fiona asked, surprised.

"Since he was a boy and his mother died, Eadan's always been duty bound; I rarely see him enjoy pleasures—including love. Since I've been ill, he's taken on even more. I'm proud of my son, but I want him tae enjoy his life as well. His rashness in marrying ye shows he's capable."

A rush of guilt flowed through Fiona at their lie, and she lowered her gaze.

"Well, perhaps he'll be very happy with Maga- idh," she forced herself to say. That woman was awful, through and through. As if reading her mind, Bran's expression darkened, and he sighed.

"He's marrying her out of duty. I feel guilt for pressuring him, but 'tis the best way for peace. Our clans have been feuding for years, 'tis the only—" He shook his head, giving her an apologetic look. "Listen tae me, burdening ye with our problems."

"It's no burden," Fiona insisted. "I can't thank you and your son enough for helping me."

Bran settled his eyes onto her, gazing at her for a long moment.

"If things were different..." he trailed off, shaking his head. "Ye can take yer leave, lass. No need tae listen tae the ravings of an old man."

"They're not the ravings of an old man," she said gently, smiling. "But I'll leave you be."

"Fiona," he said, as she reached the door. She

turned back to face him, stiffening when she saw that his expression had darkened. "If—if anything should happen tae me, will ye look out for Eadan? I ken ye're on yer way, but if ye cared for him once..."

Unease filled her. Why would Bran want Fiona, an outsider, to watch out for Eadan? But Bran was giving her a pleading look.

She swallowed, pushing aside her unease.

"I will," she said quietly, and stepped out of the room, closing the door behind her.

CHAPTER 12

*W*ith great difficulty, Eadan kept his distance from Fiona for the rest of the day; it had taken everything in his power to stop himself from kissing her earlier.

When the next morning came, he reasoned that he needed to see her to find out how her meeting with Elspeth went, yet as he stepped out of his chamber, a servant intercepted him, handing him a letter.

"What's this?" Eadan asked, puzzled.

"The steward asked me tae deliver it," the servant said.

Eadan took the note and dismissed his servant, stepping back into his chamber. He opened the letter, freezing when he read the message scrawled inside.

I know what Dughall's planning. Meet me at the rear of the stables—now. Not safe to discuss in castle.

Eadan lowered the note, his heart thundering in his chest. He'd known the steward of the castle, Naoghas, since he was a lad—he'd served as steward of the castle when his father was acting laird. Naoghas was taciturn yet straightforward; it wasn't like him to write Eadan a letter.

Why wasn't it safe to discuss in the castle? Was there a traitor among his servants? Among his clan?

He made his way out of the castle and to the stables, trying to keep his expression neutral, though panic already flowed through his veins.

When he arrived at the stables, he found them empty.

"Naoghas?"

He looked around, but there was no sign of his steward. He entered the stables and froze.

In one of the empty stalls, splatters of blood stained the ground.

EADAN CALLED for the stable boys and several of his servants, ordering them to search the grounds for Naoghas. But Eadan's instinct told him they wouldn't find him.

He returned to the castle, his chest tight with alarm. He found Ronan in his guest chamber and told him what happened.

"This was Dughall's doing," Eadan growled.

"Calm down," Ronan cautioned, though his own expression had filled with fury.

"How can I? Naoghas must've somehow figured out whatever the bastard was planning, but Dughall had him killed. I think someone in the castle's working with Dughall. Naoghas said it wasnae safe tae discuss in the castle."

"Aye," Ronan said, grim, "but we still need tae be careful. We cannae make any accusations without proof."

"My steward may be dead," Eadan snapped. "I've half a mind tae go tae Dughall and slice him through with my blade."

"Do ye want another war? We need proof it was him," Ronan returned.

"He's already declared war," Eadan bit out, but he knew Ronan was right. It would do no good to accuse Dughall without proof. He'd only mention the disappearance to the handful of nobles in his clan he trusted implicitly; they'd carry out their own investigation.

A part of him had hoped his instincts about Dughall were wrong, that he genuinely wanted peace. But if he'd killed Naoghas, Dughall was no man of honor, a man he wanted no affiliation with.

Fiona entered his mind, and panic coiled though him. Dughall didn't want her here, that was clear. Would he try to harm her as well?

"I want a guard on Fiona. Osgar or Taran," Eadan said, naming the two men of the clan he trusted. "She's not tae wander the castle grounds alone."

"Aye," Ronan agreed. He reached out to grip

Eadan's arm, his voice wavering with emotion. "We'll find Naoghas, dead or alive. And we'll bring the man who killed him tae justice."

After arranging with Ronan a time and place where he could meet with a handful of his trusted men, Eadan left to find Fiona. Relief flowed through him when he found her in her chamber, gazing out the window. Without thinking, he moved toward her as she turned, pulling her into his arms. He held her for a long moment, relief and desire colliding in his chest.

"Eadan?" she asked, blinking in surprise as he released her. "Are you all right?"

He studied her, his heart pounding, but decided not to tell her about his missing steward. It was none of her concern and it would just worry her.

"I'm just glad tae see ye," he said hastily. It was true; the sight of her was like the sun chasing away a foggy gloom. But he noticed that her brown eyes were filled with conflict. "What's the matter?"

A renewed surge of fury flowed through him when she told him of her visit to Elspeth and her encounter with Magaidh.

"Eadan, I know you say she doesn't care for you, but she seemed genuinely upset."

"She doesnae," he interrupted. "I've only seen hatred in her eyes since the betrothal was arranged, she's keeping up appearances. It would seem odd if she didnae act threatened by ye."

But Fiona didn't look so certain. She bit her lip,

his gaze lingered on the sensual fullness of her mouth, arousal surging through him as he recalled how her lips felt against his. He averted his gaze, taking a step back from her.

"And that's not all. I spoke to your father," Fiona said. "He asked me to watch out for you—in case anything happened."

Eadan stilled, his mind whirring. So his father did suspect something was amiss. Did he suspect Dughall and Clan Acheson?

"Do you think—do you think your life is in danger?" Fiona asked, her eyes widening with worry.

"I doonae ken," he said, "but I want ye to be safe going forward. If someone's targeting me, they're also targeting ye. I'm having a guard on yer door, and ye're not to go around the castle grounds on your own."

"Why?" Fiona breathed. "Eadan, has something happened?"

A knock on the door interrupted the moment, and Eadan was relieved for it; he didn't want to drag Fiona further into this than she already was. How could he let her know she need not concern herself with his matters?

He recalled how Fiona told him of her love of painting. With everything that had happened, he'd forgotten to have the servants fetch her painting materials. Anything to keep her mind off troubles that need not worry her and put the light back in those lovely eyes.

"Nothing that concerns ye," he said finally, before going to the door and swinging it open, expecting to find Una.

But Ronan stood there instead, his expression grim.

"Dughall and his men are here," he said. "He wants tae see ye."

Fury seized him; Dughall had the nerve to show up here after having his steward killed?

"Get Osgar tae stand by her door," he said to Ronan, before turning to Fiona, giving her a regretful look. "I'll be back soon."

EADAN ARRIVED IN THE HALL, frowning with concern when he saw his father gathered with the other nobles. He wanted his father to rest more, not take part in meetings, especially ones which involved the snake Dughall.

Eadan gave Dughall and his men curt nods of acknowledgment before moving to his father.

"I'll handle this," he said in a low voice. "Ye need rest. The healer said—"

"While I'm still alive, I'm taking part in meetings," Bran said, glowering at him. "I'm not dead yet, lad."

Eadan sighed. His father was stubborn; there was no use trying to get him to leave.

He straightened, moving to the center of the room. He met Dughall's eyes, who evenly returned his stare. Eadan clenched his fists at his sides, suppressing his fury.

"What's the purpose of yer visit?" Eadan asked, trying to keep his tone cordial.

"I'm here on account of my daughter," Dughall snapped. "Yer *wife* paid her a visit, and threatened her."

The nobles began to mutter among themselves, and Eadan's fury rose. So that was why Elspeth had invited Fiona over for a visit; Elspeth and Magaidh had lured Fiona into a trap. *And I encouraged the visit*, he thought, with a stab of guilt.

"My wife," Eadan said, surprised at how easy it was to refer to Fiona as his wife, "was invited tae Elspeth's home. There, she was ambushed by Magaidh and Elspeth after she insisted she wanted nothing more than tae go on her way tae the nunnery. They threatened her; she defended herself."

"Are ye calling my daughter a liar?" Dughall demanded. "May I remind ye, 'tis yer future wife ye speak of?"

Never, Eadan thought, but held his tongue.

"Until my marriage is annulled, I'll not have my wife insulted—nor threatened."

"Bran, I think yer son has forgotten he's betrothed tae my daughter," Dughall seethed. "The laird still seems quite taken with this secret wife. He almost killed one of my men for merely complimenting her beauty. That tae me doesnae seem like a man who wants—"

"Leave Fiona out of this," Eadan hissed. "I was defending her honor."

"I willnae," Dughall returned, glaring at him. "I find it very convenient that she shows up, putting yer betrothal to my daughter on hold. Ye're probably bedding the lass, filling her belly with yer bastard child."

Eadan stepped forward, fury raging through him like a blazing fire, but Ronan put a restraining hand on his arm. Dughall's eyes narrowed.

"Ye have one month," Dughall said, his voice tight with anger. "One month tae annul yer marriage and send the lass away. Then ye'll honor the betrothal to Magaidh, or our clans are back at war."

CHAPTER 13

*U*na entered Fiona's chamber not long after Eadan left, telling her the laird sent his apologies, but he was unable to join her for supper tonight and it would be better if she dined in her chamber. At first, hurt had filled Fiona, then worry. Eadan had looked troubled when he'd come to her room earlier to embrace her, and she suspected there was something he wasn't telling her.

When Una brought in her meal, she forced a smile and thanked her, though a bereft feeling had settled over her. She hadn't realized how much she looked forward to suppers with Eadan; he'd become an anchor in this time.

The next morning, Fiona awoke with a renewed determination. She needed to set aside her attraction to Eadan and focus on getting back to her own time.

She dressed and headed back down to the cellar where she first arrived, in the slim chance the portal had somehow reappeared. But it still bore the appearance of an ordinary cellar—no wind, no hint of any portal. She reluctantly left when several servants entered, giving her odd looks.

"There ye are," Una said, when Fiona returned to her chamber. Una paused from putting away laundered gowns into a chest, giving her a puzzled look. "Where've ye been?"

"Just—exploring," Fiona lied. She studied Una as she resumed putting away the gowns, a thought suddenly striking her. "Can I ask you something?"

"Anything, m'lady."

She'd just realized it was quite possible she wasn't the only person who'd fallen through time and arrived here.

Fiona hesitated, biting her lip. Una had shown nothing but kindness to her, but Fiona certainly wasn't going to tell her she was a time traveler.

"Have—have there been any disappearances nearby?"

"Why do ye ask?" Una asked, setting down a gown, her brow furrowed with concern.

"I—I've just heard gossip," Fiona stammered. She should have thought this through before bringing it up, but hastily continued, "And I wondered if you knew anything."

"Ah, most gossip is nonsense," Una said, waving it off, and Fiona's heart sank. "But," she continued, after a brief pause, "every once in a while, I hear rumors of people disappearing around the abandoned village of Tairseach, not far from here. There were even rumors of people appearing out of nowhere. Some believed 'em tae be spies, others thought they were spirits. Still others thought the *stiuireadh* had something to do with it all."

Fiona's mind was whirling as she struggled to keep up.

"The stiuireadh?" she echoed.

"Aye," Una said. "Druid witches. I admit to having my beliefs, but I've never been one for witches. There are those who believe the stiuireadh have something to do with the strange happenings around Tairseach. No one kens for sure, but many believe the village once belonged to them."

Fiona swallowed as all the air seemed to seep from the room. Druid witches? She recalled the strange woman who'd followed her in her own time. Could that woman be one of them?

"I—I thought the druids died out long ago. During the time of the Romans," Fiona said, struggling to recall facts she'd learned from an ancient history course she'd taken in college.

"That's the common belief, aye. But many think the surviving druids blended into the population, and some even had their own villages—Tairseach being one of 'em."

Fiona stared at her, her heart hammering. She

recalled the ruins of the medieval village where she'd disappeared in her own time. Maybe this village was the portal, not the cellar of the castle. And the woman who'd followed her was a stiuireadh—or a descendant of one.

A part of her wanted to burst out into hysterical laughter. Days ago, she wouldn't have even entertained such a notion. But that was before she'd traveled six hundred years into the past. Now it seemed like anything was possible.

"I see," Fiona said, trying to keep her tone casual, though it wavered a bit. "You said this village is abandoned? Where is it?"

"Oh, half a day's ride from here; 'tis in one of the more remote parts of the Highlands. 'Tis been abandoned for some time, no one quite kens why. But folks 'round here willnae risk settling there."

Fiona considered her words, her mouth going dry. This Tairseach increasingly sounded like the same village where she herself had disappeared in her own time.

But how could she get there? And another question niggled at her mind; if this was indeed the village she'd found in her own time, how did she end up so far away from it? And if that woman who'd followed her in her own time was a druid witch, did she need her to return to her own time?

Lurking beneath her excitement over possibly finding the portal, conflict loomed. Various images of Eadan filled her mind; the way his blue eyes lit up when he smiled, the seductive rumble of his voice, shaped by his Scottish brogue, the feel of his hard-muscled body pressed against hers. In her own time, Eadan was long dead. At the thought, a stab of grief pierced her, and tears stung her eyes.

"What is it, m'lady?" Una asked, looking worried. "Has someone ye ken disappeared at Tairseach?"

"No," Fiona said, blinking back her tears. "I just—I hope I'm not causing the laird too much grief by being here."

It was a flimsy lie, but she'd needed to think of something on the spot. Una's eyes softened, and she put down the gowns, stepping forward to give Fiona's hands a comforting squeeze.

"I've never seen the laird as relaxed and happy as he is around ye," Una said, and Fiona's grief dissipated, replaced by a sliver of joy.

A chambermaid entered, and Fiona turned. The maid set down a parchment and several small jars, along with a bristled brush on a side table. For a moment, confusion filled Fiona, and then she recalled how she'd told Eadan about her love of painting the night he'd taken her to look at the lands that surrounded the castle.

"He remembered," she said, beaming, as her sadness from moments before vanished completely. The parchment and jars must be medieval painting materials.

"Aye," Una said, glancing over at the materials. "Had the servants go tae the village tae fetch what we could. I was afeared he'd make us travel tae

Edinburgh tae get yer supplies." She slid a sly gaze to Fiona. "He wants tae make ye happy while ye're here."

Fiona lowered her gaze, blushing. Was Una playing matchmaker?

"He's set aside a chamber for ye tae get yer painting done," Una continued, giving her a wide smile. "What are ye waiting for, m'lady?"

Fiona trailed Una from her room and down the corridor to another large chamber, pushing aside her jumble of thoughts about Tairseach, druid witches, and Eadan.

Una told her it was a guest chamber, but Eadan had bequeathed it for her use while she was here.

When Una left her alone, Fiona looked around with awe. The chamber was as large as hers and Eadan's, but it wasn't the size of the chamber that filled her with amazement. It was the stunning view from the window.

Pressing her hand to her mouth, she stumbled forward. From this vantage point she could see all the emerald green grounds that surrounded the castle—the forests, the glistening lake beneath the morning sun, and farther in the distance, the rolling mountains and hills of the Highlands.

"Oh my God," Fiona whispered. Another jolt of déjà vu had hit her, but there was no uncertainty attached to the feeling. She knew exactly where she'd seen this landscape before.

In a painting located in an Aberdeen museum in the twenty-first century. The same painting that had struck her with strange recognition. Now she knew why that recognition had struck her, that dizzying sense of déjà vu.

It was because she'd been the one to paint it, over six hundred years in the past.

CHAPTER 14

*F*iona took several breaths to calm herself, her eyes still trained on the view. It was stunningly, breathtakingly beautiful, and there was a magic to it, a magic that somehow allowed her, a person born centuries in the future, to be here now.

She had always considered herself to be a practical person, but she couldn't shake the feeling that she was . . . *meant* to be here. That everything in her life—the death of her parents when she was a child, her distant aunt who'd given her the necessities as she'd grown up, but never a great deal of affection. Her years of loneliness, even her disastrous engagement to Derek. All of it had led her here. To Eadan. And the fact that she'd already painted this landscape seemed to point to that.

But Fiona shook her head, trying to hold on to reason. It was basic causality. She'd already traveled to 1390 by her time, so everything that happened here had already happened. Hence the déjà vu when she saw the painting. She would still get back to her own time, and Eadan would handle the danger that faced his clan and marry a suitable Scottish bride. That's all there was to it.

Suppressing a wave of conflicting emotions, Fiona set down the painting materials onto a table that was set up in the center of the chamber. This was what she needed. A sanctuary, a way of taking her mind off the bizarre circumstances she found herself in.

Well, Fiona, she mused to herself, as she sat down to paint. *You've already painted this, so it should come easy.*

She immersed herself in her painting, careful as she worked with the parchment and natural pigments, using egg yolks the servant had provided as a binder. It wasn't as difficult to work with medieval painting materials as she'd feared; in fact, it felt natural, as if she'd done this a thousand times before. And she had done this before.

Eadan's familiar scent of rosewood filled her nostrils, and she stilled, coming back to the present as he entered the room, stopping at her side. His eyes were trained on her painting. Feeling self-conscious, she set down her brush.

"No. Don't stop. It's bonnie, Fiona. Truly," he said, giving her one of his heart-melting smiles.

A swell of pride filled Fiona. Eadan was taking in her work with genuine awe.

"Thank you," she said.

"I'm sorry I had tae leave ye yesterday and I couldnae return," Eadan said, his smile fading as he rubbed his temple.

"Has something happened?" she asked, studying him with concern.

He averted his gaze, and she knew he'd evade her question. She reached out to grip his arm.

"You can tell me," she said gently.

"Dughall is suspicious of ye," he said, after a brief pause. "He made me promise tae get the annulment and send ye away within a month or the truce is off." He closed his eyes and she could now see the strain in his entire body. "Decades of fighting will resume, and all because of me. Part of me thinks I should go ahead with the betrothal and—"

"No," Fiona said, firm. She thought of Magaidh's cruelty, of Bran asking her to watch over Eadan. Something was amiss. And she knew it was selfish, but a hot jealousy coursed through her at the thought of Eadan marrying Magaidh. "You were right to listen to your instincts."

"It seems my instincts have only made things worse," he said, giving her a regretful look. "I shouldnae have dragged ye intae all of this."

Fiona stood, giving his arm a squeeze of reassurance. His blue eyes met hers, and the silence between them shifted, becoming infused with an unspoken desire.

Her mouth went dry as their eyes remained locked, and the moment seemed suspended in time, until Eadan slowly leaned forward, pressing his lips to hers.

This time there was no caution, no hesitancy. All rational thought went out of Fiona's mind as Eadan reached out to press her flush against his body. Every part of him consumed her as he plundered her mouth with his tongue—his masculine scent, the feel of his muscular torso pressed against her breasts, the hardness of his arousal flush against her center.

"Fiona," he whispered, his tone reverent, as if she were a goddess he was worshiping. "Ye're bonnie. The bonniest lass I've ever laid eyes upon."

Her heart swelled as he swung her up into his arms, bridal style; his eyes locked with hers as he carried her to the bed.

He lowered her to the bed, and she whimpered as he trailed kisses down her jaw to the arch of her throat, the swell of her breasts. He teased her, his mouth kissing the fabric of her bodice above her breasts.

"Please, Eadan," she whimpered. "Please."

He gave her a teasing smile, but he obliged, yanking down the bodice of her gown, then her tunic and underdress, until he reached her breasts. He growled at the sight, taking them in with reverence before leaning down to capture one aching nipple into his mouth.

She groaned as he suckled, her hand going to his thick wavy hair as he moaned around her breast, before turning to lave his attention on the other one. Moisture seeped from between her thighs, and she began to quiver with the promise of release.

"Not yet," Eadan whispered, finally tearing his mouth from her breasts to settle his desire-filled blue gaze on her.

He undressed her, torturously slow, before shedding his own clothes. Fiona took him in, breathless. He was as beautiful undressed as she'd always suspected—with a broad muscular torso. She gasped at the size of him, swelled and erect with need.

"All for ye, my bonnie Fiona," he whispered, before leaning forward to claim her mouth with his.

When he released her from his kiss, leaving her breathless, he trailed kisses down her chest, the plane of her abdomen . . .

"Oh, God," Fiona gasped, as his mouth clamped onto her center.

The room dimmed around her as he tasted her, his blue eyes never leaving hers, moaning his pleasure. Tendrils of hot desire coiled around her as she quaked, gripping the sheets at her sides, her breath heaving, and she let out a cry as she came, and Eadan's mouth remained clamped onto her as she trembled and quaked, before settling back down to earth.

Only then did Eadan trail kisses back up her body to her neck, and sank his massive length inside of her. Fiona let out a long moan at the hard sensation of him inside of her, and he gave her a moment to adjust to his length before he began to move, his eyes hazy with desire.

Fiona wrapped her arms around him, her fingers sinking into the flesh of his back as he thrusted, the bed pounding into the wall behind them, and everything in the room faded away. There was only Eadan and the sensation of his strong, lean body on top of her, their bodies joined in mutual pleasure, climbing toward a place of release.

"Look at me, lass," Eadan gasped, as he pounded her into the bed. "Look at me as I cum inside of ye. As I make ye mine."

Fiona's eyes locked with his, and together their bodies began to shudder, climbing to that place of pleasure where nothing else exists.

Fiona's body continued to quake as Eadan stilled, peppering gentle kisses along her jaw.

When she stilled, out of breath, her gaze settled onto Eadan. He wrapped his arms around her, keeping her body pressed flush against him as he rolled over onto his side. They lay still for a moment, the only sounds in the chamber their labored breathing.

"I've wanted tae do that the moment I found ye in my castle, wearing that sinful dress," Eadan confessed. "Ye're a siren, Fiona."

Fiona flushed as he sat up, reaching out to sweep her hair back from her face. His expression shadowed, and he expelled a sigh.

"I want nothing more than tae keep ye by my

side," he said. "But things are getting dangerous, and 'tis not right tae keep ye here."

A wave of hurt filled Fiona at his words. He seemed to sense her thoughts, pinning her with his gaze.

"I doonae want tae. I wish circumstances were different," he said, "but I'm worried Dughall—or Magaidh—will try and harm ye. And—ye mean a lot tae me. More than I realized. I couldnae bear it if harm came tae ye."

Fiona closed her eyes, a dull feeling of heartache settling over her, though she knew Eadan was right. Besides her conflicted feelings about leaving, she didn't even know if she could get back to her own time. What if the village Una spoke of was just that—a village? How would she know where to find the portal?

"What?" Eadan asked. "The nunnery should—"

"I'm not going to the nunnery."

She couldn't keep up the lie, and she didn't realize how much she wanted to open up to him until now.

When she opened her eyes, she was relieved that Eadan didn't look surprised, nor angry.

"Are ye going tae tell me where ye're from, then?" he asked, his tone gentle.

Fiona took a breath, sitting up, searching his beautiful blue eyes. It was time to tell him who she really was.

She scoured her brain for any fact she could

use to prove that what she told him was truth. And then she remembered something. She'd visited a history museum in Aberdeen a few days before she'd arrived in this time, and the guide had droned on and on about King Robert, who was king in this time. She was so glad she'd listened intently to the guide's words.

"Yes," she said. "I'll tell you. But I need you to listen to every word."

CHAPTER 15

*E*adan sat in stunned silence, trying to comprehend what Fiona had just told him.

She'd told him she was from the twenty-first century, and she'd arrived through some sort of portal in the ruins of a castle in the village of Tairseach. She used strange terms to describe the time she was from—cars, technology, airplanes—words that barely penetrated his stunned haze.

Now, her beautiful eyes were locked on his, a silent plea in their depths. Eadan had to look away from her. *Christ,* he thought. *Is the lass mad?*

Though he should have been concerned, a sense of betrayal flowed through him. If she wasn't mad, she was a manipulator. Could she be one of Dughall's spies after all?

"You don't believe me."

He forced his gaze back to Fiona. Her eyes had

filled with tears, splintering his heart. He got to his feet, tugging on his clothes with shaking hands.

"Of course you don't," she continued, her voice wavering. "I don't blame you. I wouldn't believe me either."

He turned to face her, trying to form words, but he needed to determine which Fiona was—mad or manipulative. She was the picture of loveliness, looking at him with utter sincerity in her eyes, clutching the bedcovers to her luscious breasts.

He forced himself to look away from her, clenching his fists at his side, his heart hardening. This was why he didn't have relationships; he never should have allowed himself to care for her.

"Eadan?"

"I'll arrange transport for wherever ye want tae go," he said tightly, still not looking at her. Mad or manipulator, he still wanted to keep her safe, fool that he was. And if she was indeed a spy, it was best he sent her off sooner rather than later.

"Eadan—wait—" her voice choked on a sob as he strode to the door. He faltered, his hand on the doorknob. *She's already made you weak*, a phantom voice whispered. Still, he lingered, waiting for her to continue. "I—can tell you something. Something that will make you believe me." She took a breath. "King Robert. He's ill, isn't he?"

"Aye," Eadan said, confused. Why was she bringing up King Robert? "But he's expected tae get well, and—"

"He won't get well, Eadan. Tomorrow's the

nineteenth of April. He will die, and his son will take the throne as King Robert III. I went to a history museum before I—arrived here."

"Museum?" he echoed blankly.

"It's like a library. It keeps historical records. They're common in my time," she said. "That's where I learned this." She paused, studying his tight expression. "It—it's important to me that you believe me."

Eadan studied her, a chill coiling around him. She was lucky he was not a superstitious man, and that he wasn't particularly fond of the king, who hadn't come to his clan's aid when they'd needed him in years past. It was dangerous to speak of the death of the king.

But there was something in her eyes, a keen desperation that made him hesitate. He told himself he was a fool for believing her, for falling into what could be a trap. But there was a part of him that wanted—needed—to believe her. Because, God help him, his feelings for her went beyond desire. He'd never cared for another woman the way he cared for her. And he suspected he never would.

He tried to keep his voice rough as he said, "I'm putting a guard on this door 'til I can confirm yer story. Ye're not tae leave."

Fiona paled, but she nodded. And Eadan forced himself to leave the room.

～

When he met with several trusted men of his clan in his private study, he kept the discussion centered on his suspicions about Dughall and his connection to Naoghas's disappearance. But Eadan could barely concentrate, his thoughts still consumed by Fiona and her mad story. Ronan noticed his preoccupation, giving him long looks.

After he'd given his men their orders to look into the disappearance, Ronan lingered behind. Eadan considered telling him of Fiona's story, but decided against it. He'd think Eadan was mad for even considering it.

"Ye all right, Eadan?" Ronan asked.

"Aye," Eadan lied. "I just want tae get this business with Dughall taken care of."

Ronan kept his gaze trained on him, as if detecting his cousin wasn't being truthful, before leaving him be.

It was difficult to stay away from Fiona for the rest of the day, but he needed to keep his distance until he could confirm her story.

To his irritation, Magaidh came to the hall for supper. She sat at his side, giving him a demure smile, but he could see the hatred that glinted in her eyes. Eadan clenched his teeth; he'd hoped that Dughall would keep her away from the castle.

"Where is yer wife?" Magaidh asked with feigned innocence, her eyes sweeping the hall.

"She's not well," he said tightly. He wanted to confront her about her lies to her father about Fiona's visit but held his tongue. There was no use getting her riled up, not when he was secretly investigating her father. Soon, God willing, the pretense of their betrothal would be over.

"Forgive my jealousy," she said, lowering her gaze. He could tell she was trying to appear contrite. "'Tis hard for me. There's a lass living in the castle that ye care for."

This time, when she looked at him, her eyes were almost sincere, but Eadan knew better.

"She'll be gone soon." It was difficult to say the words, and a spiral of pain filled him as he spoke them. Even though she may be mad, or a spy, he didn't want to send her away.

He managed to get through the rest of the meal, forcing himself to make small talk with Magaidh, though tension danced beneath every line of conversation. He couldn't help but compare the two: Fiona was generous and kind, Magaidh cool and manipulative. Fiona had a natural beauty that was only enhanced by her wide, open smiles, while Magaidh's beauty was severe, her smiles tight, and full of cunning. He recalled the genuine awe in Fiona's eyes as she'd taken in the landscape outside the castle; he'd never seen Magaidh look at anything that way. But there was no contest between Magaidh and Fiona—not even close. He'd never felt the slightest need and desire for Magaidh, nor any other woman, the way he felt for Fiona.

Warmth and desire swept over him as he recalled the way she'd whimpered and moaned beneath him as he made love to her. He clenched his fists at his sides, expelling a breath.

Ye need tae stay away from the lass, he told himself. *Until ye ken she's being truthful.*

But he didn't heed his own directive. After he excused himself from the table before the customary drinking began, he headed to Fiona's chamber, unable to stop himself. One of his men, Osgar, stood outside her door, and gave him a look of surprise as he approached.

"Ye can take yer leave," he told Osgar.

Fiona sat at a table in the center of her chamber, painting on a piece of parchment. She looked up when he entered, and his chest tightened when he saw the look of wariness in her eyes. Her eyes usually lit up whenever he entered the room.

"Did—did Una send yer meals in?" he asked gruffly.

"Yes," Fiona said, standing. The corners of her mouth twitched in a smile. "She gave me too much food, actually."

Eadan couldn't help but smile. Una had taken a liking to Fiona, he could tell. His smile faded as he approached, taking her by the arms and searching her eyes.

"Are ye lying tae me, lass?" He knew he was weak for asking, but he didn't want to believe Fiona was capable of such deceit.

"I wish I was," Fiona whispered. "But you'll see. Tomorrow, the king will die. Confirm the news however you can."

He searched her eyes, but he only saw sincerity there.

Eadan stayed with her that night, just holding her in his arms as she drifted off to sleep. He'd told himself he would stay away until he confirmed her story, but it was as if some force kept drawing him to her. His eyes swept over her lovely features, and his heart clenched. *What have ye done tae me, lass?*

CHAPTER 16

*I*t was late the next evening when a messenger arrived from the king's castle in Dundonald with the news that King Robert had died, and his son was to succeed him.

Eadan read the letter with shaky hands, but it wasn't surprise that filled him. It was guilt. Some part of him had known, as impossible at it was, that Fiona spoke the truth. She'd told him the truth and he'd doubted her.

He recalled with a chill a question she'd asked the night he met her. *What year is it?* With everything that happened with Dughall, he'd forgotten about that odd question; buried it in the corner of his mind. But now it came to him with the force of a sword's blow.

He tore down the corridor to Fiona's chamber. When he found it empty, panic coursed through him. Had she left and returned to her own time? Or worse, had one of Dughall's men gotten into the castle and taken her?

He turned when he heard footsteps, and relief filled him at the sight of Fiona approaching the chamber from the far end of the corridor, Ronan at her side. She stiffened at the sight of him, and the defensive look that came across her face splintered his heart.

"I needed air. Ronan took pity on me. I—"

"It's no matter," he said, striding forward to take her hand. "Ronan, leave us."

Ronan obliged him, but he saw an irritating look of amusement in his cousin's eyes as he pulled Fiona into the chamber, closing the door behind them.

Unable to stop himself, he pressed her to the door, leaning in to kiss her, breathing her in. Fiona remained stiff for only a moment before responding, wrapping her arms around him and pressing her beautiful body close to his. He wanted to hold her close to him forever, but he made himself pull back.

When they broke apart, they were both breathless. She studied him, hope filling her eyes.

"You believe me?" she whispered.

"Aye," he whispered. "Just got word from the king's castle. But even if I hadn't, I should've believed ye. I'm a fool. I should've believed ye as soon as ye told me. I'm sorry."

"You do now," Fiona said, relief flooding her

expression as she gave him a wavering smile. "That's all that matters to me."

But the elation of Fiona forgiving him quickly faded. She didn't belong in this time and he had no right to keep her here. He took a breath, forcing himself to say his next words.

"Now it's even more urgent that we get ye out of here and back tae yer own time. I can accompany ye tae Tairseach."

Conflict flared in Fiona's eyes. Eadan reached out to cup her face.

"Ye're safe in yer own time. It's tae dangerous for ye here."

Fiona bit her lip, looking as if she'd protest, but she gave him an abrupt nod.

"You're right," she whispered.

A heaviness settled over Eadan as he and Fiona slipped from the castle. They left through the rear, and he made Fiona place the plaid cloak around her head to conceal herself.

As they rode away from the castle, his tumult increased. An ache had begun to grow in his chest, one he suspected would continue to expand after she'd gone. This mysterious lass from the future had embedded herself in his heart and he didn't know how he'd remove her. He didn't want to.

Eadan tried to focus on the feel of her hands around his back as they rode, her natural honeyed scent that he hoped to memorize. He forced himself to ignore the tightness in his gut, gripping the reins with such force his knuckles turned white. Eadan had to remind himself, repeatedly, that this was for the best, that Dughall could harm her; it didn't matter that once she'd gone, his heart would return to its cage of isolation, likely never to emerge again.

They soon arrived at the abandoned village of Tairseach, and a chill crept down Eadan's spine. Like many who lived in the area, he'd heard tales of Tairseach, how people went missing here. Many believed there was dark magic at play, or that ancient druid witches had something to do with the disappearances. Eadan hadn't fallen prey to the same beliefs, but unease filled him whenever he heard rumors about the village.

But now he knew the reason for the disappearances. Tairseach was a portal through time.

Behind him, Fiona's grip tightened on him as he guided the horse through the empty village, past the old crumbling cottages and workshops until they reached the ruins of the castle on the edge of the village.

They dismounted, and Eadan tied the horse to a tree while Fiona stiffly faced the castle. She turned to glance back at the village, a look of quiet amazement on her face.

"It looked similar in my time," she murmured. She turned, pointing to the base of the castle with trembling hands.

"That's where it happened," she said. "In my time. I was following a woman, I ended up in the cellar, there was a wind—and I arrived in your castle somehow."

Eadan again cursed himself for not believing her right away. There was a genuine haunted look in Fiona's eyes.

"Then this must be the way back," he said, trying to keep his voice steady.

Fiona stiffened as she looked at him, her eyes filling with . . . pain? Longing? But the look was quickly gone as she turned back to face the castle, taking a shaky step forward.

"Do you hear that?" she breathed. "That wind?"

Eadan frowned, shaking his head. The day was perfectly still, not even a light breeze stirred the grass.

"No."

Fiona swallowed, still studying the castle. "It must be the portal."

Eadan nodded, trying to keep his expression stoic even as the ache in his heart grew. *Leave,* he silently urged Fiona. *Before I do something foolish like trying to convince ye tae stay.*

But it would be selfish to convince her to stay. He had to return his focus to gathering evidence against Dughall, finding his steward, keeping his clan safe from Clan Acheson. Fiona didn't belong in this time. Didn't belong with him.

"Then ye should go," he said, hating the way his voice trembled.

Fiona's eyes glistened with tears when she

again looked at him. She opened her mouth to say something, before falling silent again.

He stepped forward, forcing himself to give her just a brief kiss.

"Be safe and happy, Fiona," he whispered.

"You too," she said shakily, blinking back tears.

Fiona turned and approached the castle. Eadan watched her go, clenching his hands at his side, forcing himself to stay still, to not run after her . . . until she disappeared inside the castle.

He wasn't expecting the sudden pain that seared his chest like a scorching fire, and he had to expel a sharp breath and close his eyes.

'Tis for the best, he reminded himself, but that didn't ease his pain. The world around him already seemed dimmer with her absence. He didn't know if he'd ever feel the natural joy that filled him every time she was around.

He started to turn back to his horse, but froze when he saw movement out of the corner of his eye.

It was Fiona. She stalked out of the castle toward him, a determined gleam in her eyes.

"Fiona—" he began, startled.

"We made a deal," she said. "I help you, *then* you help me get back."

"Ye have helped me," he said, even as hope and delight spiraled through him. "Ye posed as my bride, and—"

"But you still don't know what Dughall's up to. We still have time before his deadline. You can still gather evidence he's working against you and your clan. I can help—by doing more than just posing as your bride. Only then will I leave. I don't know about this time, but in my time . . . a deal's a deal."

Fiona raised her head with defiance as if expecting him to protest. Admiration, joy, relief, and an emotion he couldn't identify coursed through him. He stepped forward, taking both her hands.

"Aye," he said, smiling. "A deal's a deal."

CHAPTER 17

*W*hen Fiona had entered the ruins of the castle, she'd heard the vortex of wind from its base—the same wind she'd heard the day she was transported here. But something stopped her; it was like her feet were anchored to the ground.

This is what you wanted, she'd told herself. *To return to your own time.*

But she wasn't ready to leave this time. She'd turned and stalked from the castle, determination rising within her. And while the words she spoke to Eadan were true—she did want to help him—she also knew they were an excuse. She wanted to stay with *him* for as long as she could. The connection she had with Eadan went beyond the physical; it was as if a part of her craved his presence. His deep, rumbling voice, his cerulean blue eyes, the way he looked at her when he didn't think she was aware—with not just desire, but with affection and a hint of longing. She knew in her heart she'd never have such a connection with anyone again, and it was just her luck that her perfect man was a Scottish laird from the fourteenth century.

But Fiona tried not to think of this as Eadan led her back to his horse. She leaned forward, relishing in the feel of his strong body against hers as they rode back to Macleay Castle. There was no part of her that felt an ounce of regret as the ruins of the castle and Tairseach faded into the distance behind them. Instead, as they approached Eadan's castle, she felt as if she were returning home.

Back at the castle, Eadan led her to her chamber, where he closed the door behind them.

"While I'm here, I think I should work in the kitchens," she said, turning to face him.

"Why?" Eadan asked, looking puzzled.

"If Dughall already hired one of your servants to spy, I'm guessing he's approached others. If I ingratiate myself with the servants in the kitchens they might be more apt to confide in me."

"I doonae ken," Eadan said, shaking his head. "I may treat my servants well, but they'd not be comfortable making friends with the laird's wife."

"Not friends, exactly," Fiona said, "but comfortable enough to eventually confide in me. If I ask. All it takes is one."

But Eadan still looked doubtful.

"It's worth a try," she pressed. "I'm staying here to help, remember?"

"I'm still having a guard on ye at all times,"

Eadan said, after a pause. "And ye're not tae wander the grounds alone, Fiona."

"I'll be careful," she said. "I promise."

Eadan studied her, admiration filling his expression as he shook his head.

"I doonae ken if ye're foolish or brave, lass," he said finally, stepping forward to cup the sides of her face.

"Perhaps both?" she asked, her breath catching in her throat at his nearness.

"Aye," Eadan growled, before leaning down to claim her mouth with his. Keeping his arms around her, he walked backward with her to the bed.

"Lie still, my Fiona," he whispered, and her heart soared at the possessiveness of his words. It took everything in her power to remain still as he divested her of her clothing.

When he stripped off his tunic and kilt, desire spiraled through her. His muscular torso gleamed in the illumination from the fireplace, his blue eyes hot with lust, his lips parted as he surveyed her naked body. He was so beautiful.

She couldn't help herself. Disobeying his command, she sat up, peppering kisses along the plane of his broad muscular chest, going lower, lower still, until she took his hard erect length into her mouth.

"Christ, Fiona," he gasped, as she luxuriated in the feel of him in her mouth, licking along his length, before sucking him down whole. "Ye're going tae kill me."

She smiled around his shaft, and continued to suckle him, as his hands wound through her hair, his teeth clenched with restrained lust, his eyes filled with raw desire.

"I want tae cum inside ye," he ground out, releasing himself from her mouth with great effort.

He sat down on the bed next to her, lifting her up and gently sinking her down onto his erection.

Fiona let out a pleasured moan at the sensation of him filling her, and she wrapped her arms around his neck, locking eyes with him as he clutched her rear. Their eyes remained on each other as Fiona rode him, and Eadan's hands wandered from her rear to her breasts, stroking them before pulling each aching nipple into his mouth. Fiona gasped and threw her head back, feeling the start of her orgasm spiral deep within her belly.

"Aye, my Fiona," he whispered. "Come for me, lass. My siren."

And Fiona did, her body quaking her release, as Eadan groaned his own orgasm, his grasp tightening as he spilled himself inside of her.

Fiona buried her face in his neck, still coming down from the dizzying heights Eadan had taken her to. Eadan kept her in his arms, removing himself from her as he moved to lie down on the bed. When they lay sideways, he reached out to stroke her tousled hair.

"I'm a fool tae not have thought of this before—

but we've not been careful. I doonae want tae send ye back with a babe in yer belly."

Her chest tightened at his mention of her going back to her own time, but she forced a smile.

"No need. In my time, there are sophisticated—and effective—ways of preventing women from getting pregnant."

She'd received a birth control shot for years now, though a part of her wondered if it would withstand a supernatural event such as time travel. And it would wear off in a few weeks' time. A sliver of delight went through her, just for a moment, at the thought of having Eadan's child . . . of having a real marriage with him.

But she quickly squashed the thought. Eadan had his duties as laird and soon-to-be chief of Clan Macleay. Knowing Eadan, as soon as this business with Clan Acheson was sorted, he'd marry a suitable Scottish bride. Pain struck her at the thought, and she swallowed.

When she looked back up at Eadan, she saw a flash of what looked like regret in his eyes before it vanished. She blinked. He couldn't want her to have his child . . . could he?

"Tell me more," Eadan said abruptly, averting his gaze. "About your time."

Fiona propped herself up on her elbow, thinking for a moment. How to summarize the twenty-first century?

"It's loud," she said, after a moment. "A lot louder than this time. I find the quiet here more peaceful. Technology—which I think many people in this time would equate to magic—dominates the future. It makes things more convenient. But I think it's caused less personal connections. Everyone has a device to hide behind."

He listened as she told him as much as she could about the modern age, his beautiful eyes filled with wonder. She suspected it took a lot for a rational man like Eadan to express genuine surprise, and she relished in the look of boyish wonder on his face when she described airplanes.

But his expression suddenly darkened and he propped himself up on one elbow, studying her with intensity.

"What?" she asked, startled by his sudden mood shift; it was like storm clouds shielding the sun.

"Is there someone waiting for ye? Back in yer time?" he asked.

Fiona smiled, delight coursing through her at the unmistakable jealousy in his eyes.

"No," she said. "I was engaged—betrothed to someone. But he betrayed me with another woman, and I ended it."

"He's a fool," Eadan said, reaching out to trace her face with his fingertip. "Why would any man go elsewhere when he can have this?"

His hand dropped from her face to her throat, to the curve of her breast, her abdomen. Fiona shivered with desire as his finger trailed lower, until he pressed it into her moist, aching center.

"Hold still, lass," he whispered, kissing his way down her abdomen. "I want tae hear ye scream my name."

And she did.

～

THE NEXT MORNING, when Fiona offered to help in the kitchens, Una looked so horrified that she had to restrain herself from laughing.

"Estranged wife or not, ye're the lady of the castle!" Una gasped.

"I insist," Fiona said firmly. "I want to earn my keep while I'm here."

"Earn yer keep?" Una asked, looking even more horrified. "As wife of the laird—"

"Eadan gave his blessing," Fiona said, giving her a firm look.

Una's shoulders slumped and she gave her a reluctant nod. Fiona could understand her hesitancy; social roles were much more stratified in this time.

Una looked down at the fine gown she'd been about to hand Fiona to wear, setting it down with a sigh.

"Well, we'll have tae dress ye in something a little less—fine," Una grumbled.

She left and returned with a simple dark brown gown made of wool. Fiona found it far more comfortable than the fancier gowns Una usually dressed her in, and considered requesting that she wear clothes like this more often, but she suspected that would give Una a heart attack.

Once dressed, she trailed Una into the kitchens. Before they entered, the kitchens had buzzed with laughter and conversation. But as soon as she entered, it was like a record scratching. All conversation halted and everyone turned to face her, mouths agape.

"Lady Macleay has offered her help 'til she's on her way," Una said stiffly, leveling them all with hard stares. "She's tae be treated with the utmost respect."

The kitchens remained quiet as Una led her to the head cook, a middle-aged woman named Isla who wiped her hands on her apron and kept her gaze lowered. She seemed reluctant to have Fiona do anything, but finally gave her a small tray of vegetables to chop.

As Fiona got to work in a small corner, the servants remained quiet. When conversation picked up again, it was hushed. Fiona felt like she was the strict teacher and the servants wary students. She knew it would take time for them to warm up to her, but she didn't have months for that. She'd have to figure out a way of endearing herself to them so that at least one of them would open up to her. Given how they all avoided even looking at her, she didn't know how that was going to happen.

Her thoughts turned to Eadan, and her decision to stay. Here she was, chopping vegetables in a medieval kitchen, when she could be back in her own time, taking a long bath in her bed-and-breakfast, reeling from her trip through time. But the thought of leaving Eadan made her heart constrict.

For so many years she'd kept her heart closed off, and there'd been a part of her that preferred things that way. But now that she'd seen the other side of opening up to someone, how good it felt—how could she ever go back to the way she'd been before?

But it didn't matter. She reminded herself for the millionth time that Eadan had his duties to Clan Macleay, and that's where his focus would remain.

She just knew that when she returned to the twenty-first century, she'd leave a part of her heart behind . . . with a man from another time.

CHAPTER 18

"We cannae have ye as a spy, Eadan. Ye're laird of the castle, and ye stand out," Ronan said.

Eadan glared at his cousin. He and Ronan had just met with his trusted men in his private study, and his men had just left. They were spying on Dughall and his men for Eadan, but they'd found nothing. And there was still no sign of Naoghas, dead or alive. Weary with their lack of progress, Eadan had proposed doing the spying himself.

"I could be discreet," Eadan said, raking his hand through his hair with frustration.

"'Tis a foolish idea, and ye ken it. Yer men are doing the best they can," Ronan said. "And . . . I have tae tell ye. Gossip's swirling about ye and Fiona."

"What gossip?" Eadan asked, stiffening.

"That ye seem close for two people trying tae get their marriage annulled."

"'Tis no one's business," Eadan said, avoiding Ronan's eyes. "She'll be gone soon."

But Ronan was perceptive; he trained an intense gaze on Eadan.

"What's going on between ye and the lass?" Ronan asked. "Ye can tell me, Eadan."

Eadan hesitated. He and Fiona had agreed to keep her secret to themselves. Everyone would think she was mad, and for those who didn't, they'd accuse her of witchcraft. Eadan trusted Ronan with his life, but he wouldn't divulge her secret to anyone. He expelled a sigh, deciding to tell him a half truth.

"I care about Fiona. More than I should," Eadan hedged, though his words were an understatement. Fiona had infused his world with light, with joy. He dreaded the day he'd have to part with her.

"Have ye bedded the lass?"

"That's not yer business," Eadan growled. He didn't want Ronan—or any man—to even think of his Fiona in the throes of passion.

"Ye are," Ronan said, shaking his head. "I know jealousy when I see it. I suspected yer feelings for the lass when ye attacked Uisdean. Fiona is bonnie, of that there's no doubt. But doonae let her distract ye, Dughall's—"

"I'm not distracted. I'm doing everything I can tae bring Dughall down," Eadan returned.

Ronan's mouth tightened, but he gave him a quick nod before leaving him alone.

Eadan sank down into his chair. He'd just lied to Ronan; Fiona *was* distracting him. He recalled her lush body writhing beneath his, the sweetness of her quim, his name on her lips as she came, and arousal filled every part of him. He thought of her amusement as she tried to explain the concept of a "computer" to him, her soft laughter that reminded him of bells, the determination in her eyes when she told him she would stay to help him.

Eadan rubbed his temple. It was no surprise that people around the castle noticed how he behaved around Fiona. Try as he might, he couldn't keep his eyes off her when he was in her presence.

She's still going back tae her own time, he told himself. This situation with Dughall would resolve and she'd be out of his life, forever. He imagined her in this distant future, eventually marrying another man, and his fists clenched at his sides. He forced away the thought, jealousy and pain filling him at the thought of his Fiona with another man.

Eadan made himself focus on reading papers that Naoghas had left behind regarding land requests from various nobles of the clan.

When a servant notified him that supper was being served, he pushed aside the papers, his eagerness to see Fiona so great he had to restrain himself from practically running to the great hall.

But before he could leave, Ronan entered, his mouth set in a grim line. He was holding a trembling male servant by his arm. Eadan recognized the servant as Maon; he'd worked at Macleay Castle for many years in the stables.

Eadan's eyes widened in surprise as Ronan threw Maon to the floor, glowering at him.

"What are ye doing?" Eadan demanded, glaring at Ronan. He wouldn't tolerate the mistreatment of his servants, and shock filled him at Ronan's behavior. His cousin had always treated the servants with kindness.

"This man," Ronan bit out, "was following yer wife. He admitted he's a spy for Dughall."

Fury coiled through Eadan. He reached down, dragging Maon up by the collar of his tunic, his hand going to the hilt of his sword.

"P—please, m'laird—" Maon sputtered.

"Why were ye following my wife?" Eadan snarled.

"Dughall—he paid me. Wanted me tae follow 'er—not tae harm 'er, I swear. I was tae follow 'er and report back to 'im."

Eadan's grip eased on Maon's collar—a little.

"How long have ye been following her?"

"'Tis—'tis only the first day," he said. "Please—" Maon's eyes glistened with tears. "I've a sick bairn, and we cannae afford tae pay the healer. Otherwise, I'd never've done it. Mercy, m'laird. Please."

Eadan gazed down at the man, sympathy filling him, dampening his rage. He recognized a desperate man when he saw one. He was lucky he hadn't harmed Fiona or Eadan wouldn't feel so merciful.

"How much is he paying ye?" Eadan asked.

When Maon told him the amount, Eadan swore. *That bastard,* he thought. Dughall spent that much coin to spy on Fiona?

"I'll pay ye double," Eadan said, after a pause, ignoring Ronan's curse and look of disbelief. Maon's eyes widened, as he continued, "Ye pretend tae keep spying on Fiona, but this time, ye give Dughall false information. Tell him that Fiona's eager tae leave, we keep our distance, and I suspect another clan of wrongdoing. Ye report back tae me or Ronan at the same time every day in the stables. Regardless of whether ye help me, I'll arrange a healer for yer bairn. But," he said, narrowing his eyes, "if I get word of ye telling Dughall any of this and betraying me again, I'll not hesitate tae destroy ye. Understand?"

"Aye," Maon said, looking both terrified and relieved. "I understand."

EADAN HATED TO DO IT, but he took supper in his chamber. If Dughall had more spies working in his castle, he didn't want to risk them reporting his behavior around Fiona. He wouldn't be able to mask his feelings for her, his concern.

But once it was late and the castle had gone quiet, he went to her chamber.

His heart lifted at the sight of her; she was

changing into her nightdress. She stilled at the sight of him, relief flooding her expression.

"I didn't see you at supper," she said. "I—I thought you were avoiding me."

"I was," he admitted, and a look of hurt crossed her face. "But not for the reason ye think."

He told her about the servant who'd been following her. She paled, sinking down into the bed.

"This is why 'tis important that ye're careful. I think Dughall will harm ye. Fiona," he hedged, forcing himself to continue, "are ye certain ye want tae stay? Dughall is—"

"I gave you my word," Fiona said, her eyes flashing, and another surge of admiration went through him. "A deal's a deal."

She held his gaze, and he gave her a relenting nod.

"How was yer time in the kitchens?" he asked.

She looked pleased that he changed the subject, though she sighed.

"The servants acted like frightened animals around me," she said. "I tried striking up conversations, but I only got one word replies."

"They're used tae Magaidh," he said darkly. "She treated them with contempt. Give them some time, they'll warm up tae ye."

He knew he should leave and return to his own chamber, but he'd stopped listening to logic the moment he made love to her that first time.

He approached, reaching out to stop her as she started to lace up her nightdress, heat spreading through him as he touched her bare skin.

"Ye willnae be needing tae get dressed, siren," he said gruffly, before his mouth claimed hers.

CHAPTER 19

Fiona tried to concentrate on chopping vegetables, but images from the passionate night she'd shared with Eadan filled her mind. His lips on her skin, their naked bodies fused together as he moved within her. She'd lain awake after he slipped from her room to avoid being seen in the morning, unable to stop herself from fantasizing about waking up next to him every morning.

Though she hadn't been in 1390 for long, she didn't feel as out of sorts as she had when she'd first arrived, and to her surprise, she hadn't longed for the conveniences of the future that much. Yes, sometimes she missed the internet or her cell phone. But it was refreshing to spend time painting, or walking the castle grounds, or just conversing with Eadan.

The one thing she did miss from her time was Isabelle, and her heart tightened when she thought of how worried her friend must be. As soon as she could, she would try and figure out how to let her friend know she was all right. Could she send a letter through the portal, with the hope that some wayward tourist would stumble upon the village and get it to her?

But Fiona shook aside the thought. There was no need to do such a thing, because she would return to her own time herself, where she belonged, though a sliver of dread filled her at the thought.

"Careful, m'lady," a hesitant voice said, and Fiona looked up. A young woman with strawberry blond hair and kind blue eyes, who couldn't be older than nineteen or twenty, stood there, gesturing to the knife Fiona was holding.

She looked down, blinking. She'd had been so wrapped up in her thoughts she hadn't realized how close her finger was to the blade.

"Thank you," she said, smiling. "Ah—wait," she said hastily, before the young woman could step away. This was the first time a servant in the kitchen had spoken to her, unbidden.

Fiona had listened in on the servants' conversations. It was hard to understand the thick Scottish brogues at first, but she'd now become accustomed to them and listened carefully to their discussions. This young woman, whose name was Sorcha, had a crush on one of the stable boys, but feared he wouldn't return her affections.

Sorcha froze, looking petrified. Fiona smiled to put her at ease.

"Forgive me, but I've listened in on some of

your conversations about Taran, the young man who works in the stables," Fiona said in a low voice. "And . . . I think you should talk to him about how you feel. I—I also had a crush on a man who worked in the stables when I was younger."

Fiona hated the lie, but she needed to ingratiate herself somehow. But she didn't get the reaction she was hoping for. Sorcha flushed, lowering her gaze.

"I—I'm sorry, m'lady," she said. "I ken I should be focusing on me work; I willnae speak of such matters while working, again."

Fiona looked at her, gobsmacked. She knew for a fact that Eadan treated his servants with kindness; she'd seen him invite servants to sit at his side during suppers in the great hall and inquire about their families. His father, Bran, was also kind to them. She could only guess it was Magaidh who'd put the fear of God into these poor servants.

She looked around, noticing that another hush had fallen over the kitchen. The servants avoided her eyes, tending to their tasks.

Sighing, Fiona put down her knife and moved to the center of the kitchen. Enough was enough.

"Excuse me," she said, waiting for everyone's eyes to reluctantly fall on her. "I won't be here for very long; I'm only working in the kitchens to earn my keep. I'm not your mistress—not really. Please talk freely among yourselves. I insist. Ailde, I'm glad your daughter is feeling better. I'll ask the laird if he can have extra food sent to your home. Ros, I hope you can make it to the spring festival. Laise, I do hope your crops do better when the seasons change. If they don't, I'm sure Eadan would be happy to help."

She'd picked up these tidbits by listening in on their conversations and hoped they wouldn't be affronted. For a moment, stunned silence filled the kitchens, with many of the servants looking at her with wide eyes. But to her relief, she saw many of them relax. A couple even gave her hesitant smiles.

Satisfied, she returned to her chopping table, where Sorcha remained, her eyes wide.

"As I was saying," Fiona continued, "if I were you, I'd tell Taran how I felt."

Sorcha's astonished look faded and she blushed.

"What—what did ye do?" Sorcha asked.

"About what?"

"The lad you liked?"

A wave of relief washed over Fiona and she smiled. Sorcha was warming up to her.

"I never told him," Fiona said. Unbidden, her thoughts went to Eadan, and her heart clenched. "He—he married someone else. I was broken-hearted. That's why I urge you—tell him how you feel. Before it's too late."

Again, another image of Eadan popped into her mind. The way his eyes lit up when he laughed. The look of wonder on his face when she told him about the twenty-first century.

Did she feel more for Eadan than just desire?

Did she more than care for him? At the thought, Fiona dropped the knife and drew a shaky breath. Sorcha hurried forward to pick it up, handing it to her.

"There's a faster way to chop," Sorcha said, giving her a helpful smile. "Here, let me help ye."

After that day, the servants became more relaxed around her. Over the course of the next week, their discussions were less guarded. They were still very aware of her presence, and they never discussed Eadan nor the other nobles around her, but at least they no longer treated her like she was an evil queen.

Sorcha was the one who opened up to her the most. She learned that she was the only child of an elderly mother, and she was conflicted about her feelings for Taran, as it would be better for her to marry a man with better prospects. Fiona listened, careful not to impose her modern-day opinions, reminding herself that she was in another time. Soon, very soon, she hoped to ask Sorcha if she'd noticed any strange behavior among the other servants. But she'd have to bide her time.

Eadan continued to visit her chamber every night, and she looked forward to the time they spent together; he'd tell her about his duties as laird, his slow-moving investigation into Dughall and his missing steward, and she'd tell him about her time in the kitchens. He rarely asked her about her own time anymore, and she was glad. Discussing her own time was like highlighting the ticking clock over their time together, counting down until they'd go their separate ways. She tried not to focus too much on her growing feelings for Eadan, over feelings she knew that went far beyond desire. It was too painful to dwell on, so she pushed all thoughts of her deepening feelings aside.

But after another week passed, the pressure had intensified. Soon the deadline would be up and Eadan would have to send Fiona away and resume his betrothal to Magaidh—or risk war between the clans. But Eadan hadn't come up with the proof needed to convince the nobles of his clan that Dughall was behind Naoghas's disappearance.

"I think I should go talk to Magaidh," Fiona said, when they'd returned to her chamber after supper late one evening.

"What? Are ye mad?" Eadan demanded, looking at her with disbelief.

"She hates me," Fiona said, thinking aloud. "She could barely restrain herself the last time we spoke. I think she'll slip and reveal something. Something you can use against Dughall."

"Ye'll not go tae Dughall's manor," Eadan snapped, not looking convinced by her argument. "'Tis dangerous and I forbid it."

"You forbid it?" she snapped, hot anger rushing through her.

"I doonae care how things are in yer time, but here my word is law. I willnae have ye confronting Magaidh. I—I fear for ye, Fiona," he said, his voice wavering, and her anger melted away when she saw the worry in his eyes. "Yer doing more than enough by making nice with the servants. I'll handle Dughall—and Magaidh."

But it turned out she didn't have to go see Magaidh. Magaidh came to see her.

A nervous-looking Una came to fetch her from the kitchens the next day, telling her she had a visitor.

"Who?" Fiona asked with surprise, taking off her apron as she followed Una out of the kitchens.

"Magaidh."

Fiona hesitated, her heart thudding wildly in her chest. Eadan was away from the castle with Ronan; otherwise, she'd have gone to him first.

She took a deep breath, willing herself to be calm. She could handle Magaidh on her own.

Magaidh was waiting in a large drawing room off to the side of the great hall. Her mouth tightened in dislike at the sight of Fiona, along with a look of surprise at her plain peasant dress.

"Hello, Fiona," Magaidh said. She spoke tightly as if each word were forced. "I've come tae apologize."

Fiona blinked, astonished. Magaidh didn't look conciliatory at all; hostility radiated off her in waves.

"Apologize?" Fiona echoed.

"I threatened ye. I ken ye're leaving soon, and

ye have no intention of challenging me for Eadan. I wish to offer ye my kindness before ye left," Magaidh said stiffly.

Fiona studied her. The woman was lying through her teeth. What was she really here for?

"I accept your apology," Fiona said, trying to force warmth into her tone. "I—I hope you two find happiness."

What if Eadan didn't find the proof he needed, and he ended up marrying Magaidh after all? She knew he wanted peace for Clan Macleay more than anything. The thought of Magaidh marrying Eadan filled her with both jealousy and revulsion.

Fiona swallowed, lowering her gaze. When she looked back up, Magaidh's eyes had narrowed, her fists clenching at her sides.

"I kent it," Magaidh breathed. "Ye love him."

"Wh—what?" Fiona gasped.

"It makes ye sick, doesnae it? The thought of us together. I can see it in yer eyes. I've no doubt he's bedded ye—Eadan has needs like any other man. Not that I doonae have my own lovers."

A chill went through Fiona as Magaidh glared at her—not only at her own admission of having lovers, but the pure hatred that emanated from the woman.

"Why did you come here?" Fiona asked, trying to keep her voice steady.

Magaidh let out a sharp breath, looking even more furious that she hadn't denied sleeping with Eadan. But what was the point of denying it?

Magaidh wouldn't believe her and Fiona was terrible at keeping her feelings for Eadan hidden.

"Tae see if yer lying with my betrothed."

"You are not betrothed," Fiona said through clenched teeth. "It's been put on hold since my arrival."

Though she wasn't legally wed to Eadan, she realized in the moment how *real* their faux marriage felt. How natural. It no longer felt like a charade, and a surge of possessiveness flowed through her. She wasn't going to feign niceness with this woman anymore.

"Eadan is *my* husband," she continued fiercely.

"I loved Eadan once," Magaidh said, her green eyes flashing with fury. "'Til I realized he didnae care for me. Just ken—yer not the only lass Eadan has bedded. There will be many more—if there aren't already. Doonae fool yerself intae thinking yer special tae him. I made that mistake once."

Magaidh stormed out, leaving Fiona alone, uncertainty paired with heartache settling over her like a great weight.

CHAPTER 20

When Eadan returned to the castle, frustration coursed through him. He and Ronan had questioned a man in the village they thought had information about Naoghas. It turned out the man was a drunkard just looking for easy reward money.

Eadan gritted his teeth, raking his hand through his hair. Dughall's deadline was fast approaching; he needed proof to present to the nobles, and fast.

He made his way to Fiona's chamber. Just being in her presence would calm him.

But when he found her in her chamber, seated at the table and painting, he could immediately tell that something was wrong. Her shoulders were tense, her mouth compressed in a tight line, and she didn't look up when he entered.

"Fiona?" he asked, alarmed. "What's wrong?"

When she looked up, tumult lurked in her eyes. She set down her parchment and stood.

"Magaidh paid me a visit," she said shakily. "She —she guessed that we've made love. And she mentioned having her own lovers."

Eadan closed his eyes and swore. He didn't know how Magaidh had figured that out, unless Dughall had yet another spy working in the castle.

"Fiona?" he asked, when he opened his eyes again. Fiona still looked shaken. "Did she say something else?"

Fiona hesitated, biting her lip. But shook her head.

"Well, I can only assume she's not told her father. Otherwise, Dughall would've been here by now," he muttered. "And the fact that she told ye she has other lovers—"

"Do you care?" Fiona asked, studying him closely. "That she has other lovers?"

"No," Eadan returned, frowning. Was that what she was upset about? Did she think he cared for Magaidh? "'Tis a relief. I've always kent she doesnae care for me nor this arrangement. This only proves it."

"She told me she cared for you once. That—that she used to love you," Fiona said, jealousy plain in her eyes.

Eadan stepped forward, cupping her face.

"Even if that were true—which I doubt it is— she doesnae anymore, I assure you. And I've no feelings for her. The lass makes my blood run cold. There's only one lass who has my eye," he said, his voice dropping to a husky whisper.

Fiona blanched, turning away from him.

"Fiona—" he began, surprised.

"I—I'm going to return to the kitchens," she said, still not looking at him. "I was making leeway with one of the kitchen maids. She might know something."

She left before he could stop her. Eadan frowned, watching her go. Fiona was hiding something from him, and he was determined to find out what it was.

THE NEXT MORNING he met with Ronan in his study, telling him of Magaidh's visit.

"She said something tae upset Fiona—something Fiona willnae share with me," Eadan growled. "She'll tell her father I've bedded Fiona."

"If that were true, ye know Dughall would already be here, furious. I think it was pettier than that. I think Magaidh's jealous of yer lass and wanted to unsettle her."

"Well, she succeeded," Eadan said. For the first time in weeks, he'd not spent the night with Fiona, suspecting that her chill toward him had not melted. "I'll not resume my betrothal tae Magaidh, even if we doonae find proof against her father. 'Tis a farce."

"That's not wise," Ronan said, shaking his head. "'Tis important we doonae let on we believe something's amiss. We need tae do this the official way; 'tis the best way tae avoid needless bloodshed. Our investigation may be slow, but it'll come along. We'll get Dughall by not behaving rashly." Ronan paused, shaking his head, looking at Eadan with sudden amusement. "I cannae believe I'm telling ye, the most rational and duty bound man I ken, tae not behave rashly. I think yer lass is affecting ye more than ye realize."

Eadan glared at him, though his cousin had correctly judged him.

"Bring me Maon," Eadan said, averting his gaze. He didn't want the conversation to linger on his growing feelings for Fiona. "I want tae see if he's learned anything."

"I did as ye asked and told Dughall what ye told me tae say," Maon said, moments later, after Ronan brought him to his study. "But Dughall wants me tae keep trailing yer wife."

"Fine," Eadan said shortly, "but I need ye to find out more from Dughall—any proof ye can get of Dughall's scheming. As soon as I have it, I'll send ye and yer family somewhere safe."

A look of relief and hope filled Maon's eyes, and he turned to leave.

"He's just a stable worker," Ronan said, once they were alone. "Not some expert spy. Ye cannae expect him tae—"

"We're running out of time," Eadan interrupted. "Less than two weeks 'til Dughall's deadline. We need tae do what we must for proof."

Eadan tried to concentrate on his work once

Ronan left, but his thoughts were consumed with Dughall, Magaidh's scheming, and as always, Fiona. He feared the distance she'd displayed the day before would continue, and he couldn't bear that. He needed her warmth. Needed her. He wanted to be close to her for whatever time they had left together.

Eadan froze as he noticed something out the window. He stood, moving over to it.

Outside, Fiona and his father strolled the grounds of the inner courtyard. At first, anger coursed through him at the sight. He'd told her not to wander the castle grounds on her own; his father was not adequate protection. But he relaxed when he saw one of his men, Osgar, trailing them from a safe distance behind.

He left his study to head to the courtyard. As he approached, he noticed that Fiona and his father seemed deep in conversation; Bran seemed more relaxed than Eadan had seen him in months. While Magaidh had never been rude to Bran, she treated him with a cool and distant politeness.

Fiona suddenly laughed at something Bran said, and Eadan couldn't help but smile. Genuine warmth emanated from her toward his father.

Fiona seemed to sense his eyes on her, and paused, turning around to face him. She smiled, but he saw a slight wariness in her eyes.

"I saw your father out for a walk. He asked me to join him," she said, her body stiffening, as if she expected him to reprimand her.

"Aye, I see that. May I walk with ye?" Eadan asked, turning to glance at his father.

"Ye can," Bran said, his eyes twinkling with amusement. "But only if ye can tolerate the stories I'm telling Fiona about how ye behaved as a lad."

Eadan let out an exaggerated groan as they continued to walk, and Fiona turned to look at him with amusement.

"Your father tells me you've not changed much since you were a boy. Ronan was always the playful one, you the serious one."

Eadan scowled. He'd always known that he was next in line as chief of Clan Macleay, and laird of Macleay Castle. That had placed an enormous weight on his shoulders—how else was he supposed to behave?

"Ye should spend time painting with Fiona before she has tae go. Told her I've never seen a lass who paints."

Surprise filled Eadan. He couldn't imagine himself painting, he rarely had time for leisure. But Bran had a hopeful look in his eyes, and Eadan wouldn't turn down the opportunity to spend more time with Fiona.

"Aye. I'll try," he said, meeting Fiona's eyes with a smile, but she averted her gaze. Eadan's stomach tightened; he was going to find out the true reason for her distance.

As they continued walking through the court-yard, his father's voice low as he continued to ply Fiona with tales of his childhood, he found himself

158

wishing that circumstances were different. That Fiona was his actual wife, that there was no rival clan to deal with, that he could put duty aside.

Soon, he could tell that Bran had begun to tire. He and Fiona helped his father back to his chamber. He stood back, watching with unease as Bran's maids helped him into bed; the brief walk had drained him more than it should have.

He'd not told Bran about his investigation into Dughall, nor Naoghas's disappearance and likely murder; he feared it would weaken his father's already fragile health. As he studied his father now, he decided he'd have another healer come look at him.

Fiona turned and started to leave, pulling him back to the present, but he reached out to grasp her arm, stalking with her to his chamber.

"Eadan—" Fiona snapped, twisting in his grasp, but he didn't let her go until they were inside his chamber.

"I want tae ken what's wrong with ye, lass. Ye've been acting strange since Magaidh's visit. What did she say tae ye?"

"I told you what she said," Fiona said, lowering her gaze.

"Fiona," he said gently, stepping forward. "I can read ye well. What else did she tell ye?"

Fiona seemed to deflate, closing her eyes. When she opened them again, pain filled their brown depths.

"Magaidh told me you might have other lovers.

I—I know it's not my business—I'm not your actual wife. But I think it's fair for me to know if you do."

Eadan looked at her in disbelief. How could she think he had other lovers when he had access to her beautiful body each night? The thought of bedding anyone else filled him with revulsion. He'd bedded women in the past, but he'd never had more than one lover at a time. Ronan had often encouraged him to find more lasses to bed.

But relief soon replaced his disbelief. Fiona was jealous. It wasn't because she was withdrawing from him as he'd feared. It was because she felt possessive over him.

Without a word, he stepped forward, swinging her up into his arms.

"Eadan!" she gasped, but he could see desire flare in her eyes.

"I've not looked at another lass since ye arrived in my castle, in that sinful dress," he said, walking with her to his bed. "Ye've consumed every part of me, siren. The thought of another lass in my bed fills me with ire. The thought of ye with another man," he continued, jealousy flowing through him as he lowered her to the bed, "fills me with rage. While ye're here, ye're mine, Fiona. All mine. And I'm yers."

He claimed her mouth with his as he lowered his body on top of hers. Fiona clung to him, wrapping her arms around his body. He lifted his head up, gazing into her cedar brown eyes.

"I only see ye, my siren. My Fiona."

Fiona's eyes filled with emotion. He hiked up her gown and released himself from his breeches, sinking his hard length into her, again claiming her mouth with his. She whimpered with desire as he began to move within her.

He thoroughly made love to her, exploring every inch of her lovely curves with his hands and mouth until she cried out his name.

Afterward, as they lay entwined and breathless, he wondered how he could ever live without his siren, his Fiona, who had consumed not just his body—but his heart.

CHAPTER 21

You've consumed every part of me.

Eadan's words reverberated in her mind, and Fiona felt like she was floating on air the next morning. It took all her efforts not to hum while she settled in to work at her counter in the kitchens.

Una had noticed her good mood when she'd brought in laundered clothes to Fiona's chamber, but Fiona had evaded her probing gaze, telling her that she was just looking forward to getting to the nunnery. Una had only looked amused, and Fiona wondered if she knew the true source of her joy. She and Eadan tried to be discreet, but she had no doubt that his trusted servants knew about their lovemaking—and they approved.

Fiona knew she should be more worried about Magaidh's knowledge of the true nature of her relationship with Eadan, but he'd told her he would handle it. Besides, she was too consumed with joy over his words from the night before to be concerned with Magaidh.

Don't overthink what he said, a phantom voice in her mind cautioned, and her joy dampened. She shouldn't assume his feelings for her went beyond desire. Her feelings most certainly did; the force of her jealousy over Eadan potentially having other lovers proved it.

A pleasant humming pulled Fiona from her thoughts, and she looked up from the carrots she was chopping. The humming came from Sorcha, who was smiling as she plopped slabs of meat into a steaming pot.

Sorcha looked up, met Fiona's eyes, and her smile widened.

"I took yer advice and told Taran how I felt," Sorcha said in a low voice, approaching her. "We're going tae the spring festival together."

"I'm happy for you," Fiona said, beaming. "You'll have to tell me how it goes."

If I'm still here, she added silently, her heart sinking. She tried not to dwell too much on the dread that filled her at the thought of leaving.

Fiona left the kitchens around midday, and as she headed down the corridor, she froze when she passed the pantry. Inside, she heard several hushed voices—including Sorcha's. She couldn't make out what they were saying, but it was clear they didn't want anyone to hear them.

Fiona continued walking, ducking around the corner from the pantry, out of sight. After several moments, she heard the door to the pantry swing open.

Fiona quickly stepped out from around the corner, spotting Sorcha step out of the pantry, looking shaken.

"Sorcha," Fiona said, hoping her voice sounded calm. "Can you help me with something?"

Sorcha blinked, giving Fiona a startled look before forcing a smile.

"Aye," she said, turning to follow Fiona.

Fiona led Sorcha down the corridor to the cellar, descending the stairs. Fiona looked around the empty space, making certain they were alone, before facing Sorcha.

"I heard you in the pantry," Fiona said, trying to keep her voice firm. This was risky, but it was worth a try. "I heard everything you said."

Sorcha's eyes widened, and she pressed her hand to her mouth, her eyes filling with tears.

"Pl—please, mistress," Sorcha said, and Fiona tried not to flinch. She'd lost count of how many times she'd asked her to call her by her name. "I didnae ken they were doing it, and I had no part, I swear. I only found out a few nights ago."

Fiona's heart pounded, and she swallowed. How could she get more information from Sorcha without revealing her ignorance? She decided that if she remained quiet, maybe Sorcha would reveal more on her own.

She was right. Sorcha began to speak, her words coming out in a jumbled rush.

"We all love the laird's father—I can only imagine Dughall paid 'em good coin tae do it," Sorcha said. "The poison's supposed tae act slowly —but the laird's father is becoming more ill than he should, and Dughall's furious. He wants his death tae look natural."

Fiona clutched the wall to hold herself steady, her heart picking up its pace. Of course. Dughall must have bribed the servants to poison Eadan's father. Eadan had expressed his concern to her over his father's inexplicably declining health.

"Who—who are the two servants?" Fiona asked.

"Please, mistress," Sorcha said, shaking her head, terrified. "It'll get back tae Dughall if— "

"Bran's life is at stake!" Fiona shouted, fear coiling through her at the thought of the kind older man's slow and painful death. "I'll keep you safe, you have my word. But I need to know their names."

Sorcha paused, her eyes wide with fear.

"Sorcha," Fiona said. "You can save his life. Please."

"Brice and Parlan," Sorcha whispered, her tears falling freely now.

Fiona recognized the two names. Brice and Parlan did menial tasks around the kitchens— hauling in sacks of spices and slabs of meat, assisting the cook and other kitchen staff with prepping the stews and larger meals for the great hall. They never spoke nor looked at Fiona; they seemed to avoid even being near her. Maybe this was why.

"I only ken because I saw 'em putting something in the food when they thought the kitchens were empty," Sorcha continued. "They said Dughall—and Magaidh—threatened their families if they didnae do it. Dughall already had the steward Naoghas killed, they told me. If—if Dughall finds out I told ye— "

Sympathy filtered through Fiona's horrified daze as Sorcha broke off, weeping. In this time, servants didn't have many options. Life was tough, brutal and short. This wasn't Sorcha's fault, nor the fault of Brice and Parlan. This was all on Dughall and Magaidh. Hatred filled her at the thought of them, and her fists clenched at her sides. She was glad she'd decided to stay. She wanted to help Eadan bring them down.

"Sorcha," she said gently. "I'm not angry with you. But we have to tell the laird."

"No," Sorcha wept. "I cannae lose my position —my mother'll die without my wages."

"The laird is kind; he'll not blame you."

"Please, Fiona," Sorcha begged. "Can ye—can ye get the laird's word that he'll show mercy? Then I'll tell him what I ken."

Fiona hesitated. She knew that Eadan would show Sorcha mercy, but the young woman looked terrified.

"I'll get his word," Fiona said finally. "And then I'll fetch you. You tell him what you told me."

"Aye," Sorcha said, though fear still lurked in her eyes.

"Keep working in the kitchens—nothing can look amiss. How are you getting home?"

"Taran's taking me on his horse," Sorcha said, wiping her eyes.

"Good. Be careful and be watchful. I'll send for you when I have Eadan's word."

Sorcha nodded and turned to take her leave. But she hesitated, training a worried gaze on Fiona's face.

"Ye should be careful, m'lady. Magaidh hates ye. She loved the laird once, and she's jealous of ye. I—I think she wants ye dead."

FEAR AND ANXIETY coursed through her as she hurried to Eadan's study, but an apologetic servant told her he'd left the castle with Ronan. She turned and immediately headed to Bran's chamber. There was no time to waste.

"He's sleeping, m'lady," said a surprised chambermaid, as she entered Bran's room.

"I'll just sit at his side," Fiona said with a forced smile. She'd just have to manually intercept the next meal his chambermaid brought in.

She looked down at Bran's sleeping form. He was pale, his breathing ragged. Again, fury roiled through her at the thought of Dughall poisoning him. But a surge of fear replaced her anger—if they were poisoning Bran, what were they planning to do to Eadan?

She didn't know how long she'd been sitting there when the door swung open and Eadan entered. She shot to her feet, taking his hand and leading him away from the bed, where she told him what she'd learned from Sorcha—including the confirmation that Dughall had Naoghas killed.

Eadan paled, a look of grief flashing across his face, before it was replaced by anger.

"Let's go see Una," he said tightly. "She loves Bran, and I trust her."

Fiona nodded, and together they went to see Una. They found her in one of the empty chambers directing several chambermaids. She straightened at the sight of Eadan and Fiona, shooing the maids out of the room.

"I need ye tae swipe out any meals sent to my father's rooms, out of sight of the other servants," Eadan said.

"May I ask why, m'laird?" Una asked, her eyes widening with shock.

"It's best ye doonae ken," he said, his mouth set in a grim line.

Una looked at Fiona, shaking.

"Aye," she said. "Ye have my word."

"Doonae speak of this tae anyone," Eadan said. "And Una—be careful."

"Aye," Una repeated, though she'd grown more pale. "I will."

As soon as they left the chamber, Eadan strode

so quickly down the chamber that Fiona had to practically run to catch up to him. She could see the restrained fury in Eadan's clenched fists, his rapid breathing, and tense shoulders.

"Now we go fetch Sorcha and those other two servants," Eadan said, giving Fiona a brief look. "I'm taking them tae the clan nobles, and they'll tell them what Dughall had them do. I need them tae tell me where Naoghas's body is, as he deserves a proper burial." He paused midstride, grief again filling his expression. Fiona reached out to take his hand.

"I'm sorry, Eadan," she whispered.

"Naoghas didnae deserve such an end," he said, his voice wavering. "But there's no time for grieving. I need tae tell the nobles. They've seen how ill my father's been—his swift decline. It should be proof enough."

"Wait," Fiona said, reaching out to grab his arm, halting his progress down the corridor. "Will you show them mercy? I gave Sorcha my word."

Eadan's mouth tightened, but he nodded. "Aye. Dughall's gone after several of my servants now. He's the one tae blame."

When they arrived at the kitchens, the servants all fell silent at the sight of Eadan. Fiona looked around, panic flowing through her when she didn't see Sorcha—nor Brice and Parlan.

"Where is Sorcha?" Eadan demanded. "Brice? Parlan?"

"We've not seen Sorcha since midday, m'laird,"

said Isla. "Brice and Parlan left tae haul in the sacks of barley, but they've not yet returned."

"Tell me where their homes are," Eadan said, his tone tight. "I'll send men to fetch them. I need tae speak tae each of them—'tis urgent."

Unease turned to dread in the pit of Fiona's stomach. She met Eadan's worried gaze. All three servants not returning to the kitchens was no coincidence.

CHAPTER 22

*I*t was later that evening, right before supper, that Ronan came to them with the news.

Brice and Parlan were missing; they'd not returned to their homes. Sorcha had been found, beaten and unconscious in the woods near the village. She was alive but severely injured and unable to speak, currently recovering in her mother's cottage.

Fiona pressed her hand to her mouth with a horrified look, and Eadan set his own fury and grief aside to wrap his arms around her, giving Ronan a silent nod to leave them.

Fiona pressed her face into the crook of his neck and wept.

"We'll find out who did this, and they'll be punished," Eadan whispered, stroking her hair.

"It's my fault," Fiona said, pulling back and looking at him with tear-filled eyes. "I'm the one who made Sorcha tell me what was happening. If I'd never come to this time, this wouldn't have happened."

"Ye doonae ken that," he said gently. "We both ken who's at fault here. Dughall."

Fiona didn't look comforted by this, guilt infusing her expression. He reached up to cup her face. There was nothing he wanted to do more than to comfort her, to hold her in his arms and keep her close, but he needed to put her safety—her life— above his own needs.

"I'm going tae handle this. Now that I ken he's attacked—and killed my servants—" he broke off, his voice shaking with raw grief and anger. "There's no telling what else Dughall will do. I need tae send ye back tae your own time."

"No," Fiona said, shaking her head. "I can still help. Dughall and Magaidh—"

"—Have proven they'll resort tae violence. Please, Fiona. 'Tis dangerous for ye here."

"Eadan Macleay," Fiona said in a firm tone, stepping back and drawing her shoulders rigid, "if I was determined to help you before, I'm even more determined now. Sorcha—" her voice grew husky with grief, but she continued, "—Sorcha didn't deserve to be beaten. She was frightened and only tried to do the right thing. I won't let you send me away until you've brought Dughall to justice. And for that, we still need proof."

A surge of emotion filled Eadan at the ferocity in her eyes and his heart swelled. This passionate and fierce woman had his heart. He knew he should insist that she go, but her expression broached no argument.

"Then ye'll stay in yer chamber—for now," he said, at the flare of renewed defiance in her eyes. "And I'm giving ye a dagger tae use; hide it away in yer bodice. I'm also putting men on yer door."

"But I want to help."

"For now, the best way tae help is staying out of harm's way. I'm going tae gather my trusted men and tell them what we ken, then I'm calling a meeting of the nobles. I've at least one servant I can use as proof against Dughall," he said, thinking of Maon. He'd hesitated to use Maon as evidence against Dughall, fearful that his men wouldn't trust his word when Maon revealed he'd spied for Dughall. But now he had no choice. "I cannae risk Dughall harming any more of my servants—or anyone. This ends now."

"Wait—" Fiona said, as he started toward the door. "Maybe there's something else you can try."

Eadan regarded her warily.

"What?"

THIS IS MADNESS, Eadan thought, gritting his teeth as he leaned forward on his horse, kicking the sides of his flank.

He was on his way to see Magaidh. It was Fiona's idea; she'd insisted that Magaidh indeed had feelings for him—or at least she once had—and perhaps he could use her former feelings to appeal to her humanity, to have her own up to what she and her father had done. At the very least, she could slip and provide him with information he could use.

Eadan didn't think this would work; Magaidh had already proven how cruel she was. But if there was the smallest chance he could prevent all-out war between their clans and simply bring Dughall to justice, it was worth a try.

So he'd left Fiona with two of his trusted men on her door. He'd brought Ronan with him, who also thought this was a mad idea. Eadan glanced over at his cousin, who rode his horse alongside him, his mouth set in a grim line. Ronan gave him a wary look that said: *This had better work.*

His spies had informed him that Dughall was away from his manor, so he knew it was safe for a brief visit. As Eadan dismounted from his horse, he had to quell the urge to set Dughall's manor ablaze. This was the man who'd poisoned his father, harmed and killed his servants. It would be difficult to maintain a polite façade with his daughter, a willing participant in his schemes.

The servant who answered the door looked startled and paled at the sight of him, but she led him and Ronan to the drawing room where Magaidh sat alone, working on her embroidery. He turned to wave Ronan away before stepping inside.

"Eadan," she said, dropping her embroidery in

surprise and shooting to her feet. She forced a smile, though it was tight and didn't reach her eyes. "I didnae expect ye."

Eadan took a breath, trying to school his expression to one of neutrality, though another surge of fury had seized him. She was the picture of innocence with her embroidery, a snake in disguise. She'd helped Dughall arrange the poisoning of his father.

"I'm here tae apologize," he lied, forcing the words past his lips. "I—I ken I've been distant and —and not warm toward ye since our betrothal was arranged."

Something flickered in Magaidh's eyes—a brief moment of raw emotion—before it vanished.

"Ye've been kind and treated me fairly," she said stiffly. "There's no need tae apologize, m'laird."

"I—I ken ye cared for me once. Perhaps when we were younger, and I never noticed," he said cautiously. This time, the look of vulnerability in Magaidh's eyes was unmistakable, and she lowered her gaze. "I ken ye no longer care for me, and I understand. But—but if ye did care for me once, ye can help me now."

"How?" Magaidh asked, her voice tight with suspicion.

"Ye can help our clans avoid bloodshed. I just need ye tae be honest with me."

Magaidh's eyes darkened and she straightened.

"Aye," she said. "I did once care for ye. But I could tell ye felt nothing for me. Ye never looked at me the way ye look at that Sassenach," she bit out, hatred filling her eyes at the mention of Fiona.

"Magaidh, my attentions have only been on my clan. If I caused ye hurt—"

"Doonae give me yer false sympathy. I ken ye're bedding the lass. No matter. What's done is done. We'll be wed regardless. Ye'll have your whore, and I'll have my lovers. But," she continued, her expression filling with lethal coldness, "we ken she's lying about something. I think she's a spy, perhaps for the English—or wherever she's truly from. My father willnae let yer whore leave 'til we question her more. Her lies will be discovered and she'll hang. But father is merciful. He'll give her a quick death the French way. By the sword."

Panic filled him at her words. *I should've sent Fiona away. I should've insisted.* But a cold hard fury seared his veins, quelling his panic. He wouldn't let them come near Fiona. He'd die first.

He glowered at Magaidh, revulsion filling him at her assumption that they would still wed. Dughall had declared war the moment he'd proposed this betrothal, the moment he'd poisoned his father and came after his servants. There was no more need for pretense.

He stepped forward, and Magaidh flinched at the look of fierce anger in his eyes.

"Doonae ye ever threaten the woman I love again," he growled. There a flash of pain in Magaidh's eyes at his statement, then fury, as he continued, "And yes, I'm bedding her. I want her tae be my wife for the rest of my life. Ye want tae ken why I never cared for ye, Magaidh? Because of yer cruelty. Ye're full of spite and hatred. Fiona's nothing but kindness, and that's one reason she has my heart. What ye and yer father are doing, it ends today."

He turned and stormed from the room before she could reply, fury still flowing through him. Ronan stood right outside the parlor; he'd been eavesdropping. He gave Eadan an impressed nod.

"So much for peace, aye?"

"Aye," Eadan said, as they headed out of the manor house to mount their horses. "We need tae call a meeting with the nobles once we're at the castle. Our truce with Clan Acheson is over."

As he rode back to the castle, his heart hammering against his ribcage, Eadan realized that his confession to Magaidh was the first time he'd admitted to anyone—including himself—that he loved Fiona. And he did. The bonnie lass who'd crashed into his life from the future had his heart, his body, his soul. For the first time in his life, there was something else that meant as much—more—to him than his clan. She'd forced him to open his heart, to let love in. To let *her* in. He wanted nothing more than to make her his wife in truth, to share his life with her.

But he needed to protect her. As long as Dughall was alive and after his clan, Fiona wouldn't be safe in this time.

CHAPTER 23

$\mathcal{F}$iona paced back and forth, feeling useless and angry with Eadan for making her remain in her chamber. One of his men, Osgar, had supplied her with a small dagger as Eadan promised. Now, the dagger rested in its sheath beneath her bodice, and she shuddered at the thought of having to use it.

Usually, she could calm herself by painting, and she'd considered it, but her anxiety was too great. She was also worried about Eadan. Though it was her idea for him to go see Magaidh as a last-ditch effort to avoid an all-out battle, what if Dughall had his men positioned there? What if Eadan was attacked?

She was on the verge of storming to the door and demanding that her guards let her out of her chamber when the door flew open and Eadan strode in. Relief flooded her, but she stilled at the dark and determined expression on his face.

"What happened?" she asked.

Eadan didn't reply. Instead, he pulled her into his arms and seized her mouth in a kiss. Shock and desire spiraled through her, and she was left breathless when he released her.

"Eadan—"

"It didnae go well," he admitted, gruff. "I—I told her I loved ye, Fiona."

Fiona froze. She met his eyes, and joy seized her at the certainty she saw in them, chasing all her other emotions away.

She hadn't allowed herself to believe that the depths of her feelings for him were love, wanting to keep the barriers around her heart erect, to protect herself from getting hurt. But she'd known deep down that she loved him, and some part of her had loved him since the moment she'd first seen him in the corridor outside the cellar.

She thought of the strange loneliness that had plagued her for her entire life, that sense of emptiness, the feeling that she belonged . . . *somewhere* else, but not being able to determine where that was. Well, now she had her answer. It wasn't *where* she belonged. It was *when* she belonged.

Here.

"I love you too, Eadan Macleay," she whispered.

"Fiona," he said huskily, stepping forward to cup her face in his hands, raw happiness in his eyes. "I want ye tae stay with me in this time, more than anything, but Dughall—"

"—This conflict with Dughall will end. I choose to stay, Eadan. In this time. With you."

"Are ye certain?" he asked, searching her eyes.

"Yes," she whispered. Everything in her life had led her to this moment . . . to him. "With all my heart, yes."

"My Fiona," he murmured, shaking his head. "All I want is ye. When this is over, I want tae make ye my wife. My wife in truth."

Fiona's heart soared, and she smiled through her tears.

"And I want you to be my true husband."

He claimed her mouth with his, and she leaned in to his kiss. For several moments, the world around them melted away. Dughall, Magaidh, the guards outside her door. There was only Eadan, his tongue exploring her mouth, his body pressed to hers, his masculine scent infusing her senses.

"My Fiona," he whispered, when he reluctantly pulled back. "When this is over, I'll have ye in my bed for days."

"Is that a promise?" Fiona asked, and Eadan chuckled. But his expression turned serious.

"I've called a meeting with the nobles. I'm telling them what Dughall's done, and then we—"

He stilled at the sound of multiple horse hooves entering the courtyard. Eadan and Fiona turned, hurrying to the window.

Cold dread filled her at the sight. Dughall and more than a dozen of his men rode into the courtyard.

"Oh my God," she whispered.

"Stay here," Eadan ordered, striding toward the door.

"Wait," Fiona protested. There was no way she'd remain in this room while Eadan confronted Dughall. "I'm coming with you."

"Fiona, now's not—"

"I have my dagger," she interrupted. "And there's a pantry adjoining the great hall—I can hide out of sight in there. Have a guard on me if you want, but I'm coming with you."

A look of admiration paired with anxiety crossed his expression, but he gave her a reluctant nod.

"Ye stay in the pantry," he said firmly. "And if it gets dangerous, ye get back tae Tairseach and yer own time."

Eadan held her gaze, waiting for her to agree. She did, reluctantly, but she had no intention of leaving him.

Ronan and several of his men stood outside the door, on the verge of knocking when Eadan and Fiona stepped out. Their eyes went wide with surprise as Fiona stepped out with Eadan, but she gave them a hard, defiant look, joining hands with Eadan.

"I've sent word tae the nobles. They should arrive soon. If Dughall and his men attack, they'll back us up," Ronan told Eadan as they all strode down the corridor toward the stairs. "As soon as I saw Dughall's men coming, I sent word tae Una tae get the servants out of the castle—they're leaving through the rear. And there are two men on yer father's door. But I doonae think Dughall's concerned with any of them."

He met Eadan's eyes, his implication clear. Dughall was here for Eadan. A sliver of dread crawled through Fiona.

When they reached the great hall, Eadan turned to her, raising her hand to his lips. A wave of fear swept over her; Dughall may be on Eadan's turf, but his men outnumbered Eadan's.

"Keep her safe," Eadan said, looking away from her to Osgar. "If—if I'm killed, take her out of here, get her tae Tairseach."

"Eadan—" Fiona protested, horror filling her at his words, but Eadan was already striding away from her, his shoulders tense as he made his way into the great hall with Ronan and the others.

Fiona looked up at Osgar, the man he'd left to guard her. If Eadan's order to take her to an abandoned village caused him any confusion, he didn't show it. Instead, he gestured for her to follow him, his face stoic.

They entered the pantry that adjoined the great hall, and Fiona headed to the door, opening it a crack.

From her vantage point, she could see Eadan striding toward Dughall and his men, who stood in the center of the hall, their hands on the hilt of their swords. Fiona swallowed hard, anxiety tightening her chest at the sight.

"If ye're here about my visit to Magaidh—" Eadan began, stopping several feet opposite Dughall.

"I'm here tae confront ye about yer lies. He's lied tae us all," Dughall roared, his eyes going past Eadan to Ronan and the other men. "I had a word with yer 'messenger.' He told me ye and yer cousin paid him tae pose as a messenger who went tae England tae seek an annulment from a priest. A priest who doesnae exist," Dughall said, his voice rising. "For a marriage that doesnae exist!"

Icy fear coursed through Fiona. This was the moment she'd dreaded since she'd agreed to Eadan's plan. The discovery of it all being a lie.

She couldn't let him take the fall for her. She started forward, but Osgar held her back.

"I need to help him—" she whispered, struggling against his firm grip.

"Ye're tae stay," Osgar said firmly. "Ye'll only make things worse for the laird."

That rendered Fiona still, and she returned her focus to Eadan and Dughall, her heart hammering.

"Tae make certain, I sent my own messenger down to Kington. Villagers there never heard of a Fiona, an Eadan, or a marriage between 'em in the church records," Dughall continued, with increasing fury. "Ye made up a marriage tae get out of the betrothal. Ye made a mockery out of the peace I offered."

Dughall's men let out shouts of agreement. Eadan, who had remained silent during Dughall's rant, though his body was rigid with tension, took a step forward.

Dughall's men went into protective crouches. Eadan held up his hands, palms up, but his eyes were filled with fury as he spoke.

"Aye. 'Tis true," Eadan said. Behind him, his own men, all except for Ronan, went still with shock. At Fiona's side, Osgar also froze. "Fiona came tae my castle seeking refuge. But she's not the one at fault. I forced her tae pose as my bride."

Horror rendered Fiona still. What was he doing? He didn't force her to do anything. She started forward again, but Osgar held her back.

"But I did it out of desperation. I kent something wasnae right with yer offer of peace. Ye've wanted our lands as long as I can remember. But now I understand what yer true intent was all along. Ye hired my own servant, Maon, tae spy on Fiona. Ye've been poisoning my father. When Naoghas realized what ye were doing, he tried tae tell me, but ye had him killed. When Fiona learned from my servant Sorcha that ye were poisoning my father, ye had the poor girl beaten, and now two other servants are missing."

Dughall didn't look outraged by his words or shocked by the accusations. But some of his men did, exchanging looks of confusion and disbelief. But Dughall clenched a fist at his side as Eadan continued.

"It just now came tae me why ye wanted me tae marry Magaidh. If my father dies from yer poison, I'd be chief of the clan, owner of the lands. Ronan cannae inherit as he's not a direct heir. But if I were tae die with no heir . . . the lands of Clan Macleay would go tae my wife and her family. The same lands our clans have been feuding over. Magaidh cared for me once, but she'd not hesitate tae poison me after we wed. That's why ye didnae try harder tae put a stop to me and Fiona, though ye must have known we were bedding. It would foster yer daughter's jealousy, make it easier for her tae kill me when it came time."

By the look on Dughall's face, Fiona could tell that Eadan had guessed correctly. Anger and disbelief roiled through her; she recalled the look of pure hatred on Magaidh's face as she confronted her. She had no doubt that Magaidh was capable of killing Eadan.

"My father is bedridden; yer poison has made him ill, and he cannae be here because of it. I'm glad he cannae see this. Ye are the one who made a mockery of the peace my father tried to sow with ye. Yer scheming and yer killing of innocents ends now, Dughall."

Dughall's features contorted with rage, and he withdrew his sword.

"When ye die, I will take control of yer clan. I'll bed yer Sassenach whore, then find out who she truly is," Dughall roared.

Dughall's words seemed to shatter Eadan's barely contained control, and the two men charged at each other, swords outstretched.

As the men in the hall began to fight, Osgar turned to her.

"Stay here," he ordered, then darted out of the pantry to join the fight.

Adrenaline flowed through Fiona as she reached for the dagger tucked in her bodice. She was no match for the burly Highlanders fighting in the hall, but if it came down to it, she'd do what she could to help Eadan.

Fiona abruptly stiffened when she sensed someone in the pantry behind her. But before she could turn, a firm hand went around her waist and a dagger was pressed to her throat.

"Doonae move, ye Sassenach bitch," Magaidh's furious voice hissed in her ear.

CHAPTER 24

ury surged through Eadan as he lunged toward Dughall, but several of Dughall's men surrounded him in a protective circle.

Eadan heard a snarl behind him, and whirled as Uisdean, one of Dughall's men, the same man he'd attacked for the lustful way he spoke of Fiona, charged at him. Uisdean raised his sword, and their blades clashed as they began to fight.

"After Dughall's done with yer Sassenach whore, I'll take my turn with her," Uisdean hissed.

Eadan's simmering rage roared to an inferno, and he let out an enraged growl as his movements quickened, but Uisdean matched each of Eadan's moves with his own. When Eadan missed a vital parry, Uisdean lunged forward, aiming his sword right for Eadan's heart. Eadan dodged just in time, but lunged forward, sinking his sword into the man's belly.

Uisdean let out a pained roar, sinking to the floor, his sword clattering to the ground. His eyes fluttered shut, but he was still alive, his breathing pained and ragged. Eadan would not kill a man who couldn't fight back, but it took everything in him not to spear him through with his sword for threatening Fiona.

But there was still fighting to be done. He turned, searching for Dughall through the mass of fighting bodies. He located him at the opposite end of the hall, his sword clashing with Ronan's.

Eadan darted toward them and joined his cousin in the fight. Dughall was an expert swordsman and he easily fought them both, his movements filled with rage. When two of Dughall's men joined the fight, edging him and Ronan to the back wall of the hall, Eadan realized with growing panic that several of his men were now injured or dead; Dughall and his men outnumbered them and were on the verge of overtaking them.

He didn't know if the nobles Ronan had sent for would arrive in time, but his worry wasn't for him, or his clan. It was only for Fiona. He could only pray that she'd heeded his words and fled the castle to get to Tairseach. He couldn't bear the thought of what would happen to her if she was here when he fell to Dughall's sword.

The thought gave him a surge of renewed strength and determination. His movements quickened, the blade of his sword clashing with Dughall's as he lunged forward. Dughall's eyes glinted, the hatred in them raw, and Eadan wondered how Dughall had maintained his civility around him for so long.

Dughall's men closed in on Ronan, and his cousin gave him a reassuring but fierce look as he turned to take them on, leaving Eadan to fight Dughall on his own.

Dughall lunged forward, aiming the tip of his blade to Eadan's throat. Eadan evaded, barely, but the blade nipped at his skin, and blood seeped from the wound.

"Where shall I enjoy yer Sassenach whore after ye fall tae my sword?" Dughall taunted, again swinging at Eadan's throat with his sword. "In the same bed ye had her? Perhaps here in the hall where I killed her treacherous lover?"

Eadan was barely managing to evade Dughall's slashes. He knew Dughall was baiting him with his words, and it was working. The fury that seared his veins made his grip tremble on the hilt of his sword, and he struggled to focus.

Dughall was fast, his aim dangerously precise. Eadan darted a quick look around the hall—Ronan and his men were too occupied fighting Dughall's men to come to his aid.

Eadan tightened his grip on the hilt of his sword, willing himself to focus, to not let Dughall's threats about Fiona sway him. He had to make the next swing of his sword count.

"Or perhaps I'll take her in each room of the castle before my men take her. Perhaps I willnae have her hanged. I'll keep her as Clan Acheson's own personal whore."

As soon as Dughall spoke, two things happened. The nobles Ronan sent for burst into the hall, descending on Dughall's men and taking out their swords. And the rage that filled Eadan at Dughall's words spurred him toward Dughall—he couldn't stop himself if he tried. Eadan lunged forward with his sword, moving faster than he ever had during a fight. Dughall may have been an excellent fighter, but Eadan had an advantage—his relative youth.

Dughall's eyes widened as Eadan's blade made contact with the flesh of his abdomen. Eadan pierced Dughall with his sword, knocking Dughall's sword out of his hands as he sank to the floor.

When Dughall was on his back, Eadan stepped forward, pressing his blade to Dughall's chest.

"Do ye surrender, Dughall?" he growled, struggling to restrain himself from killing the man. "'Tis the right of Clan Macleay tae bring ye tae justice."

Dughall glared at him, and despite his pain, the hatred remained in his eyes.

"Never," Dughall spat, clutching at his bleeding abdomen. "Clan Macleay doesnae deserve its lands nor its property, and ye doonae deserve tae be laird."

Eadan clenched his teeth, pressing his blade harder to Dughall's chest. The threats Dughall had made toward Fiona swirled through his mind, and he fantasized about spearing Dughall straight through with his sword, letting him bleed slowly and painfully to death.

But when he looked up, he saw that much of the fighting had ceased. The nobles who'd come to their aid had helped wound or slaughter Dughall's men.

He looked down at Dughall, clenching his fist. The fight was over. And as much as he wanted to kill the old man, he was laird and soon-to-be chief of the clan. There was a process the clan underwent for bringing men to justice, one that he would follow.

Eadan stepped back, tearing his gaze away from Dughall as Ronan approached.

"Imprison Dughall and his surviving men in the tower," he said. "Have a healer tend tae the injured."

But as Ronan nodded, turning to Eadan's men and gesturing for help, Dughall reached for his discarded sword in a surprisingly quick move for an injured man. He weakly lurched to his feet, still clutching his bleeding abdomen, and slashed out with his sword, aiming for Eadan's heart—

Ronan turned, letting out a horrified shout, but Eadan dodged Dughall's attack. Before he could swing again, Eadan lunged forward, sinking his sword into Dughall's chest.

Dughall stumbled to his knees as Eadan pulled out the sword. He wheezed, fighting to breathe, before falling to the floor on his side, his eyes wide and unseeing.

"Damned fool," Eadan snarled.

"'Tis for the best," Ronan muttered, as he reached Eadan's side, his breathing still ragged with tension. "When we imprisoned him, the bastard would've kept plotting yer demise from his cell."

Eadan nodded; Ronan was right. Dughall's hatred ran deeper than he'd thought.

As his men rounded up Dughall's surviving men, Eadan hurried to the pantry adjoining the great hall, searching for Fiona. But when he didn't find her inside, panic swept over him.

He stepped out into the corridor, on the verge of ordering his men to search the castle grounds for Fiona, when he heard a pained scream.

He froze, icy dread clawing through his chest. It was Fiona's voice.

Whirling, he raced down the corridor in the direction of the scream, tearing up the winding staircase. When he reached the top, he found Fiona and Magaidh at the far end of the narrow corridor, right by the window, slashing at each other with their daggers. Magaidh attacked Fiona with the ferocity of a feral cat, while Fiona's moves were more defensive; she was trying to ward her off.

Eadan charged toward them and Magaidh turned, her eyes widening at the sight of him. She grabbed Fiona from behind with surprising strength, dragging her toward the window at the end of the corridor.

"Magaidh—no!" he cried, his panic swelling as he scrambled to them.

"Ye just should've wed me, Eadan!" Magaidh cried. He'd never seen her so unhinged; her green eyes feral, her breathing coming in frantic gasps. "Ye—ye should have loved me, not this whore!"

"Stop this, Magaidh!" he pleaded, as Magaidh reached the window, still clutching Fiona, who struggled to release herself from Magaidh's grip. "All will be forgiven. Just—let her go."

"Ye'll have me imprisoned—or send me off tae a nunnery!" Magaidh spat. "Things were well before she showed up here. She needs tae die."

"No, Magaidh," he said, trying to keep his voice calm.

Fiona met his eyes, and he saw something in them that gave him pause. Though she looked terrified, there was also a determination lurking in their depths.

He realized that her struggles were just a show. She was using her free hand to slowly move her dagger toward Magaidh's leg. *Keep her talking,* her eyes said.

"'Tis my fault. I—I should have told ye my doubts about the betrothal," he said, returning his focus to Magaidh, his heart hammering frantically against his chest. "Doonae blame this on Fiona."

"Ye never—" Magaidh began, but in a quick move, Fiona slashed at Magaidh's leg. Magaidh howled in pain, releasing her grip on Fiona.

But before Fiona could dart out of her reach,

Magaidh again grabbed for her, and shoved her out of the open window.

Fiona let out a startled, terrified cry, reaching out to Magaidh to break her fall, and they both tumbled out of the window.

No, Eadan thought, horror roiling through him. Fiona wouldn't survive such a fall. *Please, God. No.*

But just before he reached the window, Fiona shakily pulled herself up over the ledge, and he almost stumbled to his knees in relief.

She turned, reaching her hands out the window, and he realized she was helping Magaidh get back inside.

He joined her, finding Magaidh clutching onto the ledge. As he and Fiona reached for Magaidh, she let out an enraged snarl, reaching up with one hand to attempt to pull Fiona out the window. But she lost her grip, slipping from the ledge and tumbling to the ground below with a scream.

Fiona stumbled back from the window, shaken, and turned, burying herself in his arms. Eadan held her close, his heart still hammering with remnant panic and fear.

"'Tis over," he whispered, stroking her hair. "'Tis over, Fiona."

She looked up at him, tears and relief filling her eyes.

"I thought—" she whispered. "I was afraid you wouldn't survive. And then Magaidh dragged me up here and attacked—"

"Ye fought well," he said. "She was determined

tae kill ye. And I wanted tae survive—for ye. We still have a life tae share, Fiona."

Fiona blinked back her tears and gave him a tremulous smile.

"I love you, Eadan," she whispered.

He leaned forward, pressing his mouth to her forehead, her jaw, her lips.

"And I love ye, my strong, brave Fiona. Always."

CHAPTER 25

One Month Later

"Ah, Fiona," Una breathed, taking her in. "Ye look bonnie."

Fiona turned to take in her reflection in the mirror Una had brought in to her chamber. Wearing white for weddings was still centuries away, so she'd chosen a gown made of blue silk that Una had ordered from a seamstress in Edinburgh. At Eadan's request, she wore her hair loose around her shoulders.

She smiled at her reflection, a rush of joy filling her chest. Today was the day she officially married Eadan.

The events of the past month had gone by in a blur. The members of the Acheson clan who'd confessed to taking part in Dughall's plot had been exiled or imprisoned; the men who murdered Naoghas were sentenced to death by Eadan and his nobles. The servants who'd served poisoned dishes to Bran—Brice and Parlan—were found in a nearby village; they'd fled out of fear. Eadan pardoned them when they returned to the castle for questioning; they'd acted under duress since Dughall had threatened to kill their families if they didn't follow his orders.

Eadan had learned through the various confessions from members of Clan Acheson that his instincts were right; Dughall intended to have Magaidh kill him after they were wed and inherit his lands. Dughall then planned to marry her off to one of his men, essentially giving Clan Acheson dominion over Clan Macleay. Members of the clan who were cleared in involvement for the plot had sworn an oath of fealty to Clan Macleay. Bran had officially stepped down as chief, Eadan was now chief of the clan. Eadan told her he believed that with Dughall gone, the two clans had finally found peace.

While Eadan was dealing with these clan matters, Fiona had visited Sorcha in the village on a daily basis. Eadan had arranged for a healer to tend to her daily, and she fully recovered from her injuries after two weeks. During Fiona's last visit, Sorcha told her with happy tears in her eyes that Taran had proposed marriage, and they would wed at month's end.

After leaving Sorcha's cottage, she'd written Isabelle a long letter, one she hoped would reach her in the present. Fiona didn't want to risk delivering it herself, she was still unsure how time travel worked. She feared that if she went through the portal again, she'd not be able to return to this time —to Eadan. And that wasn't a risk she was willing to take. She planned to leave the letter in the portal, hoping that it would reach Isabelle in the future via the next person who stumbled upon Tairseach. In the letter, she'd told Isabelle not to worry, that she was happy and to not look for her. She purposefully kept it vague; there was no way she could tell Isabelle she was in the fourteenth century without Isabelle assuming she'd lost her mind. She also hoped that Isabelle wouldn't think it was *too* odd that her letter was written on parchment. But it was the best she could do under the circumstances.

Together, Fiona and Eadan had traveled to Tairseach to deliver the letter. As they approached the castle, Fiona had heard the sound of wind—the portal. She made Eadan hold her hand as she made her way to the ruined cellar to drop off the letter, fearful that the portal would pull her through time. But nothing happened, there was no tug on her body like before. Still, she hurried out of the cellar with Eadan, tightly clutching his hand.

When they returned to Tairseach the next day, the letter had vanished. Relief filled her, and she prayed that it had been sent through time, that some other wandering tourist would find the letter and send it to Isabelle's Chicago address.

As she and Eadan left Tairseach for the final time, she thought about that mysterious woman who'd followed her in her own time. She suspected she was indeed a stiuireadh, one of the rumored druid witches Eadan and Una had spoken of. Eadan told her no one knew much detail about their magic, so she could only guess how she'd factored in to Fiona's arrival here. Maybe she was a guidepost, leading travelers like her to the past. After all, if Fiona hadn't seen her in the ruins of the castle, she'd never have entered them.

But that didn't explain Fiona's urge to take a right on the forked road that led her to Tairseach in her own time. She'd finally accepted that she'd probably never know how this all worked. Now, she could only feel gratitude; she was right where she belonged.

Going forward, she would help Eadan run the castle, continue painting, and even train young would-be artists from the village. She looked forward to her life here.

"I want tae wed ye, formally," Eadan had told her, when they returned to the castle. "I want everyone in the castle, the village—in Scotland, tae know ye're my bride."

Fiona grinned, joy washing over her at the love in Eadan's eyes.

"All right," she said, leaning forward to kiss him. "I just have one request."

He'd thought her request was odd, but he'd granted it. She wanted to marry him in the cellar where she'd first arrived. It was a meaningful location for them—it was where she'd first arrived in this time, where she'd first heard his voice, where she'd taken the first steps toward her fate of being with him. Una and the other servants had spent the past two weeks transforming the cellar into a celebratory space, and she couldn't wait to see what they'd done with it.

Now, Una squeezed her hands, pulling her back to the present.

"Are ye ready, m'lady?" she asked, beaming.

Giving her a wide smile, Fiona nodded, and she trailed Una down to the cellar.

As Fiona entered, she gasped. It had been completely transformed. There were no more sacks of barley or jugs of ale and wine. Instead, white flowers decorated several long tables that were set up along the walls. A multitude of candles illuminated the space, giving it a hazy, romantic glow. Bran, Ronan, Sorcha, Taran and a dozen other nobles and servants alike were gathered. Bran gave her a kind smile as she entered, and she returned it. She'd feared that Bran would want a suitable noble Scottish bride for his son, but Bran had told her that all he wanted was Eadan's happiness—and Fiona made him more joyful than he'd ever seen.

Fiona's gaze found Eadan, standing in the center of the cellar next to a priest. Her breath caught in her throat; he looked achingly handsome in his dark tunic and belted plaid kilt. He may have been laird of Macleay Castle, chief of Clan Macleay, but in this moment, he was simply the man she loved. The man she couldn't wait to start her life with.

His blue eyes lit up at the sight of her, and everyone else in the room faded away as she approached him. Their eyes remained locked as they spoke their vows, and when the priest announced they were wed, Eadan cupped her face with his hands, his eyes filling with emotion. He leaned forward to claim her mouth with his, sealing their future with a kiss.

CHAPTER 26

*R*onan stood at the back of the great hall, watching as Eadan and Fiona danced, their eyes trained only on each other. The guests had moved from the cellar to the great hall for a feast to celebrate Eadan and Fiona's marriage. He watched Eadan's broad smile as he swung a laughing Fiona around in his arms. He'd never seen his cousin so happy, Eadan had been too serious and duty bound before Fiona entered his life. He was glad to see Eadan allowing joy into his life, especially after the ordeal with Dughall.

His gaze slid to Fiona, who blushed as Eadan leaned forward to whisper something in her ear. He could tell the lass was kind and genuine, and he suspected nothing nefarious about her. But he suspected there was more to Fiona than Eadan had told him. Ronan had prodded Eadan to tell him where Fiona had truly come from, but Eadan's expression shadowed.

"I'll tell ye one day," he'd said, his tone somber. "But I'll doubt ye'll believe me."

Eadan had changed the subject when Ronan tried to press, and refused to further discuss the matter.

"He's happy."

Ronan turned to find Bran at his side, leaning on his cane. Ronan straightened, looking around for a chair, but Bran politely waved him off.

"There's no need—I'm off tae my chamber. This old man needs his rest. I'll soon retire tae one of the Macleay manor homes; Eadan and his bonnie bride will have no need of an old man lingering once they start their family."

"They love ye, Bran," Ronan protested. "They'll not want ye tae go."

"'Tis not up tae them," Bran said, shaking his head. "I'm no longer laird, no longer chief. 'Tis time for me tae retire, tae take in the air and rest. After this mess with Dughall and Clan Acheson..." A look of regret flashed across his eyes. Ronan knew that Bran felt guilty about all that had happened, wishing he'd listened to Eadan's warnings about Dughall.

"Ye couldnae have kent," Ronan said. "I didnae believe Eadan when he told me his suspicions. 'Tis over now. We have peace."

"Aye," Bran said, after a long pause. "I expect ye'll be called upon tae take over some duties for Eadan, now that he has a wife." Bran turned to study him, his eyes twinkling. "Soon it'll be time for ye tae find a bride."

"'Tis not my nature tae settle for one lass," Ronan said, with a dismissive wave of his hand. "I've no need of a wife."

Ronan had never desired a wife nor permanent mistress before. He'd never felt anything more than a passing fancy for a lass, and that suited him just fine.

Bran laughed, throwing back his head. He shook his head, mirth shining in his eyes.

"I once said the same thing before I met Eadan's mother. And Eadan spoke the same before he met Fiona. I cannae wait 'til ye meet the lass who changes everything for ye."

Ronan scowled, but Bran gave him another amused look, patting him on the shoulder before turning to hobble out of the hall.

Ronan pushed aside Bran's words, his frown deepening. Bran may have been the closest thing he had to a father, but he didn't know him at all. Ronan enjoyed his freedom—and he would continue to do so. He scanned the hall, taking in the various lasses. Many of them were bonnie, but none caused a fire in his belly. A surprising pang of envy pierced him as Eadan and Fiona stopped dancing to kiss, ignoring the playful cries and jests from the guests around them. It was as if they were the only two people in the hall.

"M'laird?"

Ronan turned, frowning at the sight of one of his servants, Gavin, from his manor house.

"What is it?" Ronan asked, stiffening with alarm. "Did something happen at the manor?"

"No," Gavin said, looking hesitant. "But—the steward spotted a strange lass wandering the grounds."

Read Ronan's Captive (Highlander Fate Book 2) now. Keep reading for a brief excerpt.

RONAN'S CAPTIVE PREVIEW

As Ronan drew closer to her, his mouth went dry. She was by far the bonniest lass he'd ever seen— hair the color of burnished gold, a heart-shaped face with a generous mouth and eyes a deep green that reminded him of a verdant meadow. She was tall for a lass, her slender curves pronounced beneath the lavender gown she wore. He felt himself harden against his kilt as hot, molten desire filled every part of him.

Christ, Ronan, he scolded himself. *She's an intruder on yer lands. Now's not the time tae think with yer cock.*

"Who are ye?" he demanded, once he reached her. "Why are ye intruding on my lands?"

The lass just looked at him, a stricken look in her eyes. Her gaze flitted past him to the manor and back to him. She swallowed but said nothing.

"I'm going tae ask ye again, lass," he said, stepping forward, close enough to inhale her scent—

cinnamon and rosemary. He ignored the swell of desire that surged over him, keeping his voice firm. "Who are ye and why are ye intruding on my lands?"

"My—my name is Kara," she stammered. "I'm —I'm from the—er—the village. I'm lost."

Ronan went still as he studied her. She had the same strange accent as Eadan's wife Fiona. His suspicion spiked as his gaze raked over her gown. The village was some distance away on foot, and her dress was that of a noble woman's. Noble women didn't live in villages—they lived in manor homes or castles. And they certainly didn't go around unescorted. The lass was lying to him.

"I'll ask ye again, lass," he growled. "Who are ye?"

"I told you," she said, her voice firmer now, her chin jutting upward with defiance. "My name is Kara, and I'm from the village. I'm lost. Could— could you point me in the right direction?"

Ronan's eyes narrowed. More lies. He stepped forward and took her arm in a gentle but firm grip. She let out a yelp as he dragged her toward the manor, struggling to get out of his grasp.

"Let me go!" she shouted. "This is—HELP! Let me go!"

He shot her a look of disbelief as they continued toward the manor.

"Ye're trespassing on my property, lass," he growled. "No one will help ye except me. And I willnae be doing that 'til ye tell me who ye are."

He continued to drag her into the manor, past the small group of servants who'd gathered in the entry way, keeping a firm grip on her arm as he led her up the stairs and into a guest chamber at the far end of the hall.

Only then did he release her, closing the door behind him and leaning against it with his arms crossed.

Kara stumbled back from him, looking around at the chamber like a frightened deer. Ronan's anger subsided; she seemed genuinely frightened.

"I'll not hurt ye, lass," he said gently. "I'm Ronan of Clan Macleay, laird of this manor. Now I ask ye only for the truth. Who are ye?"

"I told you—"

"The truth."

Kara blinked, and her eyes glistened with tears. His heart softened with that sympathy, but he reminded himself of the ill omen he'd received the night before. How could it be mere coincidence that she'd shown up the morning after he received it? He needed to be on guard.

"All right," she said, taking a deep breath. "I'm —I'm here to look for my family."

He studied her. He suspected she was still withholding something, but this statement seemed truthful.

"I—I arrived at a village. Somehow, I made a wrong turn, and I ended up here. I'm—I'm sorry I trespassed on your grounds, but I didn't know where I was. I just—I just want to be on my way."

"Yer family? What are their names?"

"Suibhne and Orla," she said. "They're farmers. They have two young daughters."

Ronan searched his mind, but the names were not at all familiar, and he knew dozens of the villagers by name. Her face fell, which confirmed for him she was telling the truth—at least about searching for her family.

"I'll need tae confirm yer telling me the truth," he said. "And then . . . perhaps ye can be on yer way."

"Perhaps?" she echoed, stiffening with alarm.

"Aye."

"And until then?" she demanded. "You can't mean to keep me prisoner here?"

"As ye were trespassing on my property, 'tis my right," he growled. "'Till I can confirm what ye say is truth . . . ye're my captive."

ABOUT THE AUTHOR

Stella Knight writes time travel romance and historical romance novels. She enjoys transporting readers to different times and places with vivid, nuanced heroes and heroines.

She resides in sunny southern California with her own swoon-worthy hero and her collection of too many books and board games. She's been writing for as long as she can remember, and when not writing, she can be found traveling to new locales, diving into a new book, or watching her favorite film or documentary. She loves romance, history, mystery, and adventure, all of which you'll find in her books.

Stay in touch! Visit Stella Knight's website to join her newsletter.

Stay in touch!
stellaknightbooks.com

Made in the USA
Middletown, DE
07 June 2019